The Quarterback Sneak

Little Hondo Press
Contact: littlehondopress@yahoo.com

The Quarterback Sneak
Copyright © 2014 Elizabeth Matis
Print Edition
Digital ISBN: 978-0-9840098-9-3
Print ISBN: 978-0-9908848-0-4

Editor: Karen Dale Harris
Cover Design: The Killion Group

Also by Liz Matis

Playing For Keeps – print, eBook, and audio book

Going For It – print, eBook and audio book

Huddle Up – print, eBook and audio book

Love By Design – print, eBook, and audio book

Real Men Don't Drink Appletinis – eBook

Praise for Liz Matis

Love By Design

RT Book Review: Readers will get a kick out of these characters as they walk through a world of fashion and celebrities and soak up all the glitz and glam that a wild child and a bad boy could possibly provide.

Love on the Book Shelf: Don't hold this book too tight-you-you'll burn your fingers. It's also the perfect just-before-bedtime reading, if you'd like some nice, sultry dreams.

ReRead: Totally worth it.

Playing For Keeps – Fantasy Football – Season 1

RT Book Reviews: Playing For Keeps is entertaining … an engaging storyline will keep readers turning the pages … readers will enjoy the unfolding relationship and anticipate the sequel featuring the secondary characters

Book Junkie: In Liz Matis' latest from Little Hondo Press, Playing For Keeps you will get a wildly sexy romance with depth and laughs. A page turner, bring on the sequel.

Going For It – Fantasy Football – Season 2

RT Book Reviews: Readers will wholeheartedly enjoy the cat-and-mouse game the main couple plays. Expect a large dose of spice, surprises, and a story that's perfect for the front page of a tabloid. The sequel to Playing For Keeps is a touchdown!

Book Junkie: I loved GOING FOR IT because falling hard and fast for two witty, feisty and completely honest characters that do nothing if not capture your heart and take you on the wild ride that is their love story.

The Quarterback Sneak

Fantasy Football – Season 4

Liz Matis

I see

her,

the real her

beyond what the world thinks

yes,

in my eyes, she is

beautiful

wild

but,

with my heart, she is

love

everything

mine

I see with my heart

Liz Matis – as told to by Liam McQueen

Chapter 1

Liam McQueen knew he shouldn't be inside Martini Madness or any place that served alcohol. Two years, one month, three weeks, five days sober. And celibate. Though going without a drink had proven more difficult than laying off the women. Alcohol had been his mistress, and he still heard the siren calling to his weak soul. He fortified himself with a prayer as he maneuvered through the club.

Three of his offensive linemen surrounded him, fiercely guarding their quarterback's body as if they were still on the football field. Tonight Liam was returning the favor, protecting his teammates as their designated driver and general all-around babysitter. It wouldn't help the New York Cougar's upcoming season if one of them landed in jail.

Upon reaching the club's swanky VIP section, his buddies beelined for the decorations—the pretty women let inside as bait to lure wealthy men into dropping serious cash. Liam had his fill of groupies and party girls. Deserted, he found an empty bar stool and looked around.

The glass-enclosed area allowed the music to filter in at a level that encouraged conversation, yet let the wannabes outside the glass feel like they were part of the scene, where D-list celebrities mingled with pro athletes.

From his spot, Liam had a front-row seat as he watched his largest lineman fumble a play on a hot redhead. Poor schmuck. Maybe he should help Murphy out and be his wingman for the night.

"What's your poison?" asked a sultry voice from behind the neon-lit bar.

Poison. Liam almost laughed at the truth in the word. The name of his favorite Scotch burned on his tongue.

Spinning his stool back around, he faced the bartender, a hot blonde with big boobs spilling over her low-cut shirt. She flashed him a smile bright enough for a whitening-toothpaste commercial. Three years ago, he would have simply nodded toward the nearest bathroom, and faster than it took him to call an audible on a play, they would have been going at it like a pair of drunken monkeys. His former self disgusted him.

All he wanted now was a nice girl to settle down with. A nice girl who liked sex, he amended.

"Red Bull," he said.

"With?" The suggestive hint in her voice left no doubt of her interest in him.

"Designated driver."

"Bummer."

"Yeah, it sure is." But if he hadn't gone off the wagon after single-handedly losing the Championship seven months ago, then he wouldn't take a drink now. Not even the daily reminders of defeat—fans who taunted him on the street—could break his resolve. His response at least seemed to shut them up effectively. *You're right. I suck.*

The New York fans were a fickle bunch. With a single throw, they'd forgotten how after Todd, the Cougars' star quarterback, had broken his leg, Liam had stepped in to lead them to the big game. Would the Cougars have won the Championship if Todd still had been the quarterback? According to social media, the answer was a resounding *yes*.

Apparently the team's management agreed. Otherwise Liam wouldn't have had to compete with Romer, the Cougars' number-one draft choice, for the starting position. A competition Liam had won. For now.

And he couldn't even celebrate with a toast.

Turning his head toward a commotion at the VIP entrance, he expected to see a major celebrity. But it was just another washed-up reality star. The team owner's hellion of a daughter, Hayden Middleton, had arrived with her entourage in tow.

An off-the-shoulder red cocktail dress hugged the tabloid darling's every curve, like she was channeling a plus-sized Jessica Rabbit. Even her long, cinnamon-brown hair was swept to one side. Wearing ridiculously high heels, she probably could meet Liam's six-foot-three gaze head on.

He swiveled his stool, resting his elbows on the bar rail behind him and watched her approach. *Damn.* She was going to walk right by him like he didn't exist. "Hey, Hayden."

Without missing a beat, she turned her head. "Hey, loser."

"Ouch." He grabbed his chest as if she'd struck him in the heart with an arrow. Yet it wasn't her comment that stung. Those robin's-egg-blue eyes landed a sucker punch to his gut every time she looked his way.

As she strolled by him, his gaze dropped to her sashaying backside. The judge should have sentenced the spoiled brat to a good solid spanking instead of yet another probation. His cock hardened painfully at the thought of carrying out her punishment himself. Hayden starred in his fantasies way more often than he'd like. Okay, so maybe staying celibate was more difficult than staying sober. One always seemed to fuel the other.

Where the mind leads the body will follow, he reminded himself and he looked away. At this rate, he'd be praying for salvation tomorrow instead of focusing on football practice. And when it came to Hayden Middleton, he'd be consorting with the devil's handmaiden. Not that consorting was the problem. The woman hated him, which he supposed made things easier. Less *tempting…*

Dear God, he wanted a drink. *A Scapa Scotch.* Wanted to swirl the autumn-gold liquid, inhale the honeyed fragrance, savor the sweet smoothness, feel the cool burn down his throat and then the blessed relief as the warmth spread to every part of his body.

As he glanced at Hayden again, he crushed the empty Red Bull can, then deliberately looked away. He liked to think he had mastered his addiction. That he had control. Sometimes he'd order a drink and then walk away from it, thinking he'd won a small battle of what would be a lifelong war.

A sudden roar of voices jolted him out of his pity party. His teammates were egging on two men who were nose to nose, shouting at each other, and there was Hayden adding her two thousand cents in. When the shorter guy's suit jacket flapped open, revealing a gun, Liam tossed a hundred dollar bill on the bar. *Time to go.*

In a flash he reached his unaware teammates. "We need

4

to get out of here." He placed a hand on Hayden's shoulder. "You too," he told her.

Elbowing him in the gut, she tried to wedge herself between the two guys. She shot Liam a look that made it perfectly clear that she could take care of herself. Besides, it was her entourage causing the trouble. None of that mattered, though. He owed her father for giving him a second chance when no other team in the league would.

Out of the corner of his eye, he caught a glimpse of the shorter guy's hand reaching for the gun. "Out," he ordered again.

This time his teammates took off.

With no time to argue, he threw Hayden over his shoulder in a fireman's carry. Tuning out her protests, he plowed toward the exit while doing his best to ignore the bodacious booty inches from his face. There was going to be hell to pay.

And Liam couldn't afford the price.

Chapter 2

"Put me down!" The ignoramus carrying her didn't comply. Hayden wasn't sure if Liam McQueen was simply ignoring her, or if he couldn't hear her over the blaring music in the main area of the bar. She screamed again and wiggled her body, beating her fists against his back.

This earned her a hard smack on the ass. *Oh!* Rather than offend her, the sting sent tingles of pleasure straight to her so-not-a-lady parts. This wasn't happening. Hayden Middleton was not being carried through the upscale Martini Madness Lounge like a sack of jiggling potatoes. And she was not enjoying it. *Well, maybe a little.*

As Liam stepped outside, the warm night breeze whooshed up her dress, causing the tingles to intensify. The paparazzi's flashbulbs lit up like a night at the Oscars. Her father was going to kill her. At least she was wearing panties. Screaming at Liam now would only create a bigger scene, so she remained silent.

A loud pop sounded. *Gunfire?* Then another pop. *Holy shit, definitely gunfire!*

Liam broke into a run, and her stomach bounced up and down on his shoulder, until he placed his large firm hand on her ass to steady her. She imagined him reaching up beneath her skirt with those talented fingers. Now she wiggled for a different reason.

"Saving the princess, McQueen?"

"Someone has to," Liam answered.

Upside down, she couldn't see which of her father's players waited for them near Liam's Hummer. Her fat ass must have slowed him down considerably.

"Now will you put me down?" she demanded. She was no lightweight. And as much as the quarterback irritated her, she didn't want him to throw out his back. Yet, another thing for her father to blame her for.

Liam set her down and buzzed the locks open. "Everyone, get in."

She didn't need to be told twice. If the judge found out she'd been anywhere near a gun—never mind an active shooting—her probation could be revoked. And Hayden wouldn't be caught dead in a prison jumpsuit. In her world, orange was *not* the new black.

She took the front seat beside Liam while the other three—Hondo, Murphy, and Moore—squashed into the back. A bit of guilt nipped at her conscience, but they were used to being in close contact, in the huddle or on the line protecting Liam. Besides, her ass was probably as big as any of theirs.

"Buckle up," Liam said.

She rolled her eyes, but complied. "Okay, Boy Scout."

"Maybe," Liam said tightly as he screeched away from the curb, "if you were more of a Girl Scout, then we wouldn't be in this predicament." The two cop cars speeding by in the opposite direction wailed, punctuating his point.

He was, of course, referring to her many run-ins with

the law and authority figures in general. That didn't mean she had to like what he said. "Did I say Boy Scout? I meant Dad."

A couple of laughs sounded from the backseat.

Hondo, the Cougars' center, leaned forward. "Excuse me for interrupting this amusing foreplay, but what the fuck is going on?"

"Hey, there's a lady present." Liam peered at the rearview mirror.

Hearing snorts from the back, Hayden shot the three linemen a nasty side-glance. Then she turned to Liam. "But really, what the fuck *is* going on?"

"You'd know better than me. All I saw was the runt of the litter reaching for a gun. Knew we had to get out of Dodge, so to speak."

The runt would be her brother's idiot friend, Franko. What was he doing with a gun? She knew the guy had a Napoleon complex, but a gun?

"Okay, so where to now? Another bar?" Hondo asked.

"Good idea, Honcho," Hayden said.

"It's Hondo."

"Whatever." Since the embarrassment of her father banning her from the owner's box last year, she pretended she didn't know all the names of the players, acting as if they were as interchangeable as her shoes. But in fact, she knew every name, every stat.

"I think we've had enough excitement for one night," Liam said.

"Okay, Dad." Raucous laughter followed Murphy's jibe.

Hayden couldn't suppress a giggle. She peeked over at

Liam as he concentrated on the pothole-infested New York City streets. The QB was definitely not interchangeable. The lights from the dashboard shone off his wavy reddish-brown hair, and his eyes sparkled like her favorite chocolate-diamond necklace.

Her gaze traveled down his body. He was more farm-strong than weight-room bulky. Unlike the typical tall and lean quarterback type, he had the frame of a tight end, still tall, but all solid, thick muscle with corded forearms and biceps meant for baling hay. And for throwing wayward heiresses over his shoulder.

"What?" Liam asked, leveling a gaze her way.

Caught staring, she stumbled over a question. "So what bar is it going to be?"

"I'm taking you home."

She looked out the window to see that he was indeed heading to her place along Central Park. "Are you crazy? The paparazzi will be swarming my building."

"Too soon. There's no way word got out yet."

"Oh, they'll be there. And your caveman tactics will be on the front page of all the morning papers."

"A caveman would've dragged you out by your hair." He flashed her a wicked grin. "I much preferred my way."

Heat bloomed in her cheeks as catcalls and whistles sounded from the backseat. She couldn't remember the last time she'd blushed.

The Hummer approached her building and, as she expected, a crowd of the usual paparazzi-suspects lay in wait. She should have moved after her reality show ended. Everyone knew where she lived, including Liam. *Hmmm.* Had he watched *Hayden's Place?*

"How the heck did they find out so fast?" he muttered.

Hayden snorted. "The bloodsuckers have a network that the NSA would envy."

He turned his head and smiled at her. Not a wicked grin or a challenging smirk, but a genuine smile.

Her body felt like she'd taken a shot of tequila. Shock and then a nice warm feeling. Considering she hadn't had a drink in six months, it was a welcome substitute. She had to be sure she didn't become addicted to the feeling. The sooner Liam dropped her off somewhere, the better. She'd made enough poor decisions that landed her in the press. She didn't need to make another one with her father's quarterback.

Not that she didn't crave the limelight like an attention-starved child. But for once, she'd like to be in the news for something positive. The charity work she did meant squat. The media wasn't interested in the good Hayden Middleton, and neither were men.

"Drop us off at Chancey's," Moore said. "It's only a few blocks over."

Liam sighed. "Promise you'll call the car service the team provides?"

Moore lifted four fingers. "Scout's honor." Another round of laughter filled the Hummer.

"You're doing it wrong." Liam held up three fingers, but then put his thumb and pinkie finger together.

Hayden's eyes widened. "You really were a Boy Scout?

"Eagle Scout." He pulled up to the curb by Chancey's awning and velvet rope. His gaze swept her body. "But that was a long time ago."

"Yeah, well, I was a Brownie for two seconds." She

flirted back, knowing he was harmless.

"Two whole seconds?" he said with another glance her way.

Harmless? She sucked in a breath as the full effect of Liam's smile devastated her insides. Lucky for her, he was now busy with the guys. The players filed out of the back, ribbing him with vulgar comments.

"Don't do anything I wouldn't do," Hondo said as the final jab.

Liam shook his head. "You wouldn't even know what to do."

She laughed, but the smile died on her lips as Liam turned back to her. "Where to, princess?"

The way he said the last word made it sound more like a term of endearment than a dig at her pedigree. Maybe he'd dropped off the boys because he wanted to be alone with her?

"Do you want me to drive you to your father's place?"

The mention of her father jolted her out of her misguided fantasies. "Good God, no. Take me to a hotel."

"I'm not leaving you at some random hotel. It's not safe."

Hayden considered telling him that the Ritz was right down the street, but she sort of liked this side of him. Dare she admit she liked being rescued? Wrapped in the cocoon of the car, she watched his profile as he drove, feeling safe and protected from the world. Probably some primitive gene left over from the Paleolithic age, like storing fat. A gene she had in spades. Though Liam didn't seem to have a problem with hefting her over his shoulder.

"What about I take you to one of your friends' places?"

he asked.

She checked her phone. Not one of them had answered her texts to see if they were all okay. Then again, they were probably in too much trouble with the cops to worry about her. Not that any of them *ever* seemed to worry about her. "You mean my fake friends?"

"I know what that's like."

Hayden bet he did. You didn't find out who your real friends were until there was nothing left to take. Who'd been there for Liam when he reached rock bottom? She'd seen the reports on TMZ and ESPN. Las Vegas debauchery spiraling downward ending with those awful photos of him in a hotel room with an empty bottle of whiskey and supposedly nothing left except the clothes on his back. Six months of rehab followed, along with his rededication to his Christian faith.

She wondered how dedicated, especially once she realized the Hummer was now in Tribeca. He had an apartment there, something she'd heard or read somewhere. It wasn't as if she'd done any snooping about him since he'd pushed her onto the dance floor at Angel and Billy Burner's wedding. *Well, maybe a little.* "Where are we going?"

"My place."

She scowled, disappointed that he wasn't the saint he portrayed himself to be. Was he so easily led astray?

"I have a second bedroom."

"Great." Her scowl deepened. Now she was disappointed about him *not* being so easily led astray.

At his apartment, Liam was all business. Unlike the utilitarian loft or man cave she expected, he led her through a cozily decorated space. He pointed out the second bedroom and adjacent bathroom—matched in autumn tones of warm brown and reds. He asked if she wanted something to eat from the pristine, Shaker-style kitchen. The perfect host. It annoyed her. So did his polite manner. "Well, aren't you a regular Martha Stewart."

"Back to the old Hayden, I see." He folded his arms, clearly frustrated with her. "That didn't take long."

"Wait." He had gone out of his way to keep her out of trouble. She said the second hardest thing for her to say. "Thank you."

"Wow, a thank you from Hayden Middleton."

"A 'you're welcome' would have sufficed." She tried to brush by him so she could head to the guest bedroom.

"Hold on." He stepped in her way. "I'm sorry. That was uncalled for."

He looked so contrite that she felt bad for being bitchy. Surprising herself, she said the number-one hardest thing for her to say, never mind admit. "I'm sorry too."

"For what?" He stepped closer, his breath mingling with hers.

"For calling you a loser."

"I've been called worse. I've been worse."

Did he really buy into the hype that he was to blame for the Cougars' loss last winter? "It wasn't your fault, you know?" She touched his arm. "The Championship?"

His fingers brushed along her check. "Aw, Hayden, I could kiss you for that."

Then why don't you? Hayden could melt into his smoldering eyes. Swim in them. Drown in them. She closed her eyes and willed a kiss out of him.

Instead cold air replaced his warm breath. A chill settled in her bones, and she opened her eyes and wrapped her arms around herself. "But—"

"That dress looks uncomfortable for sleeping. I'll get you a shirt to borrow." A gaze full of indecision lingered for a moment, and then he headed to his bedroom.

She didn't want his shirt. She wanted to be naked. Skin to skin. If the bulge in his pants was any indication of his interest, he did too.

So what the hell just happened? What did she do wrong? She was *nice* to him. *Nice.*

But it seemed even reformed bad guys wanted a bad girl. And Hayden knew how to be bad. Real bad. And real naughty. As soon as he came back she'd kiss him until he threw her over his shoulder and tossed her onto his bed. Only she never got the chance.

"Catch." From the hallway he tossed her his clean practice jersey.

Unprepared, it landed on her head. "Chicken," she called out.

"Jezebel," he shouted back then shut his door.

She stamped her foot and headed for the bathroom.

Chapter 3

Instead of craving a drink to start his day, Liam hungered for Hayden's pouty lips. He contemplated the closed door to his guest bedroom. Was she still in there, snuggled under the covers? Or had she snuck out at some point? With his morning hard-on poking through his boxer briefs, straight toward her door, like a compass pointing north, he dared not check.

A knock sounded at the front door. Liam grabbed a pair of sweatpants and pulled them on. He silently cursed at the badge being waved in front of the peephole. Effective as a dousing of cold water, it cured him of his erection.

He opened the door to a pair of plainclothes cops. "What can I do for you, officers?" He had the feeling they weren't collecting for a police charity drive.

"Mr. McQueen, we'd like to ask some questions about last night." They introduced themselves as detectives Ortiz and Addison. "We understand you were at the club—Martini Madness?"

"Sure." Scratching his day-old beard, he led them to the living room.

"Shots were fired," explained Addison.

The detectives declined a seat and began rattling off questions. They seemed mollified by his answers. Perhaps this was a formality. After all, Liam didn't even know the names of the guys involved. And no one was hurt. Thank God.

"What about Hayden Middleton? She was there too?" Ortiz asked.

"Yeah, but she left with me." Not exactly voluntarily, but the less Liam said the better. Was lying by omission a sin?

Ortiz nodded. "Do you know where we can find Ms. Middleton now?"

Both detectives surveyed the living room. Were they looking for evidence of her presence? A $5000 purse? A stray high-heeled designer shoe? A lacey push-up bra tossed over a lampshade?

"Mr. McQueen?"

"Uh…"

"Here I am, officers." Hayden swept into the living room, wearing only his jersey.

The fabric fell loosely about her shoulders, breasts, and waist. Fortunately the hem reached mid-thigh, big and long enough to cover her world-famous hips and ass. His hand burned from the memory of slapping those sweet cheeks. Sweat broke across his brow. *Please, God, let her be wearing panties. And please, God, erase these sinful thoughts from my mind.*

God, was no help. So Liam recited his other bible, the team's playbook, in his head while Hayden charmed the detectives and answered their questions like Entertainment Tonight was interviewing her.

"Liam, did you offer these gentlemen coffee?"

Now, she was acting liked she lived here. Stunned, he stuttered, "Ah, no… I can go make some."

"No, thank you," Ortiz said. "We're done here, for

now."

"Could I get an autograph for my son?" Addison asked sheepishly. "He's twelve."

The detective wanted a sexpot's signature for his pre-teen son? For a second, Liam was stunned. Then he realized the officer was looking at him. Liam happily scrawled out a note and signature while Addison explained the boy's dreams of someday making it to the pros.

Hayden smiled and chatted with Ortiz as if she entertained police officers everyday.

"Ms. Middleton, take good care of our quarterback."

"Oh, I will," she promised as she walked the detectives to the door.

It was on the tip of his tongue to explain that this wasn't what it looked like. Only he couldn't figure out what it was.

"Please, tell me you're wearing panties," he said as soon as she closed the door. He had to know.

Hayden twirled, arms out to display his jersey, and then she faced him, her blue eyes full of mischief and mayhem. Hands on her hips, she asked, "Why don't you come and find out?"

Her saucy grin heated his blood. He should have known better than to ask. Been a better man than to objectify a woman's body, let alone the boss's daughter. "Don't tempt me, Hayden."

"I wasn't much of a temptation last night," she pouted.

"Oh, you were a temptation alright. I'm a Christian, not a saint."

She arched an eyebrow. "Well, then, as far as you know, I'm wearing panties. In fact, big, loose granny panties."

His laughter bellowed out. 'Thanks, that helps. A lot."

"Good." But as she passed by him, she looked up at him with that seductive Jessica Rabbit come-hither glance. Oh, he wanted to hither all right. He turned his head, unable to look away. When she tugged up the jersey, giving him a view of a full moon, the beast inside him howled.

In Sodom and Gomorrah he'd be a pillar of salt right now. Instead he turned to stone—or at least one body part did.

When Liam arrived at practice, a selection of newspaper front pages and tabloid-site copies plastered the locker room walls. One headline read: *The Saint Saves the Sinner.* Another one read: *McQueen Rescues the Socialite.*

Various photos caught different angles of them coming out of the club. One, he noted, proved that she did have panties on at some point. Not that it mattered—the thong did little to hide her luscious booty cheeks.

Jake Miller, the running back, said in a falsetto voice, "Oh, Liam, you're my hero."

Liam laughed it off, ready for more digs.

Digs that were good-natured, that is. "I didn't know you were that desperate for the starting position," blasted Romer, the rookie quarterback.

The kid seemed to forget that Liam had won the spot days ago. Silence filled the locker room as his teammates waited for his reaction.

Liam almost felt sorry for Romer. The kid probably thought he'd walk right onto the field and be the star. He'd thought wrong, and now the rookie had a chip on his shoulder. In the past, Liam would've knocked it off. Now, trying to be a better man—a man of God and a man of peace—he let it go. Holding up two fingers he said, "Peace be with you, my brother."

"Fuck that," said Miller. He pushed Romer into his stall full of cleats and equipment.

Afterward, the rookie suffered through a brutal practice as Liam's teammates made it clear who the Cougars' leader was. Liam felt pretty good about that as they headed to the showers.

Until the coach yelled over to him, "The old man wants to see you, McQueen. At his corporate office. Get moving. Traffic's likely to be brutal, and Middleton hates to be kept waiting."

Crap.

Would he get a bonus for rescuing Hayden or a pink slip for taking her back to his apartment?

Chapter 4

L iam hesitated by the open door. With an ear to the phone, Marcus Middleton waved him into his stately office at the Wall Street headquarters of Middleton Nuts. Like many tycoons, the owner of the New York Cougars had his tentacles in multiple companies. Some made him richer, others, like the football franchise, were for his pure amusement. Everyone knew the billionaire toyed with his team like a kid playing Stratego.

While Liam stood off to the side admiring a display case of antique guns, terms like margins, options, and IPO flew over his head. He knew farming, football, and the Bible. And women. Rephrase that, he knew his way around a woman's body. No man could claim to know how a woman's mind worked. And Hayden's brain was in a class all by herself. It didn't matter that she was trouble, Liam still desired her.

"Just do it." Hayden's father slammed down the phone and looked up. His expression softened from a stone-cold businessman to a good ole' boy. "Hello, son, take a seat."

Son? Liam slid into the leather wingback chair in front of the imposing oak desk.

"I'll get right to the point." Middleton turned the computer screen toward Liam. "My daughter spent the night at your place."

23

Liam eyed the photo that a gossip website had posted of Hayden leaving his building. How had the paparazzi known where to find her? He'd never been bothered outside his place in Tribeca before. Wearing last-night's dress, Hayden's cat-ate-the-canary grin suggested they'd done all the things he'd wanted to do and more.

Shifting in his seat, he said, "Sir, I was only trying to help her out. She needed a place to stay."

"You expect me to believe that?"

"Yes, sir, I do." Liam's palms began to sweat.

"Then explain this." Middleton double clicked and another picture of Hayden opened on his screen. "She tweeted this to her followers. Millions of them."

Suppressing a smile, Liam examined the selfie tweeted from his guest bathroom. She looked so darn cute in nothing but his jersey that he couldn't be pissed. Instead an unexpected wave of possessiveness hit him in the gut, as if the jersey marked her as his.

The picture's setting wasn't incriminating—but the included text was.

Spending the night at McQueen's #hottie #epicnight

No wonder the paparazzi had buzzed around his building this morning.

"What do you have to say for yourself?" Middleton's fierce gaze settled on Liam.

The hashtags didn't help his cause, especially the last one. Liam scrambled for the words to explain. He tugged on his collar for some breathing room. "Sir, I know it looks bad, but I swear, she slept in my guest bedroom."

Middleton leaned forward in his throne-like chair.

"What is wrong with you, son? Don't you find Hayden attractive?"

Stunned, Liam took a moment to answer. What man wouldn't think she was hot? He remembered a year ago when her spread in *Maxim's* 100 Hottest was plastered around the locker room. He'd been torn between staring at her and wanting to rip down the pictures, then Middleton walked in and nearly stroked out yelling at his players. Sure she'd gained a couple of pounds since, but in all the right places. Places Liam wanted to explore with his hands. His mouth. His—

Not the kind of thing a father wants to hear. "She's beautiful," he said simply.

"I'm relieved you think so. That will make this less awkward."

Where was this conversation going? "Make what less awkward?"

"Your engagement to my daughter."

Liam shook his head, sure that he heard wrong. "What?"

"You heard me. The judge in Hayden's case wasn't happy that she was at the scene of a shooting last night."

"But she didn't do anything. She wasn't even drinking, and no one was hurt." Had he just defended Hayden Middleton?

"Regardless, this morning Judge Mayer was preparing the paperwork to revoke her probation. He intended to send her straight to jail for violating her court agreement."

"Intended?" *Past tense?* Liam felt relieved and uneasy at the same time.

"After I spoke with Judge Mayer, he had a change of

heart. That's where you come in, son. He expressed worry about the Cougars' season and Hayden's possible bad influence on my quarterback."

Liam might as well have abandoned her at the bar. He hadn't saved her from anything. He'd made things worse. So why was Hayden's father now smiling at him?

"I'm not sure which the judge loves more," Middleton continued, "football or his church. He backpedaled when I explained what a *good* influence you are on her. He was delighted to hear that she was out celebrating her engagement to her born-again boyfriend last night."

"But that's not true."

Middleton shrugged. "A technicality. We'll make the announcement later today. You're the perfect solution to Hayden's problems."

How could he decline without insulting his boss? He eyed the gun collection. "Sir, with all due respect, arranged marriages are not part of God's plan."

"Adam and Eve were an arranged marriage."

He knew the billionaire had a God complex, but, wow, did he just say that?

"You'd be lucky to marry my daughter." Middleton gave him a hard stare as if waiting for him to disagree. "But I'm not expecting that. It's a temporary engagement, just long enough to satisfy the judge until Hayden's probation is over."

How would he explain it to his mother? To God? "I can't agree to that either, sir."

"You can and you will." Middleton pointed a finger at his star quarterback. "You owe me. I gave you a shot when no other team would even look at you again."

Liam stood up. "I paid you back on the field. I got us to the Championship."

"Bullshit! That's why you get a paycheck, McQueen."

No more *son,* Liam noticed. Hesitating, he sat back in his chair. Was his boss right? He'd torched bridges that couldn't be rebuilt. He wasn't even sure if he'd been signed to the Cougars for his skill or because Middleton liked seeing his team in the news. Last season, Liam's battle with Todd for the starting position had fueled a legendary war of dueling headlines. Then the QB speculation had relit after the Cougars chose Romer as their first-round draft pick this past spring.

If Liam agreed to the fake engagement, the paparazzi would be crawling up his ass again. And the sportswriters? He'd be lucky to field a single football-related question after the game on Sunday. All because he'd hustled Hayden out of a bar. *Truly, no good deed goes unpunished.*

"So what's your answer, McQueen? Are you going to live up to your obligation to me? My daughter needs your help."

Liam felt like the sacrificial lamb in Middleton's family drama. But he was no lamb. He was a Cougar. He opened his mouth—

Then Middleton stopped him cold. "Doesn't Hayden deserve a second chance too?"

It could be argued in a court of law that Hayden Middleton had had more second chances than any human alive. She'd made a fortune off of being bad. Her reality show, clothing and makeup line, along with a perfume aptly named Sinfully Yours, were all built on her party-girl image.

But really, what had she done that was so awful? Yeah,

she'd spit on an undercover cop, resisted arrest and disturbed the peace. And, of course, that wasn't her first brush with the law. But she'd never been pulled over for a DWI. She'd never gambled away all her money. She'd never presented herself as a role model. Liam had done all of those and more.

The number of people he had let down—starting with God—could fill a football stadium. His dead father, his mother, his pastor, his teammates, his coach, his agent, and the fans. He felt sick when he thought about how many kids had wasted their allowance on a number seven Arizona jersey with "McQueen" emblazoned on the back.

He had messed up for real. With Hayden, he wondered how much of her antics were for the camera. Publicity was good for business. And when it came to business, she was her father through and through.

Or maybe she wanted her father's attention?

Liam tensed at the memory of his own father. "And Hayden has agreed to this engagement?" he asked slowly.

"Not yet. I had to make sure I could count on you." Middleton lit a cigar. "I won't trust my daughter to just anyone."

Did he forget that Liam was a recovering alcoholic? Or that Hayden's lifestyle could be a danger to that sobriety?

Liam couldn't ask, or his boss would lose his faith in his ability to lead the Cougars. "An engagement would be a huge distraction to the team. What about the Championship?"

"My daughter is more important than any Championship."

Maybe you should tell Hayden that. If her father had, maybe she wouldn't be in this mess.

Liam looked inside himself to hear God's word. Only silence answered him.

Was he really thinking of saying yes? Maybe the alcohol had destroyed more brain cells than he thought.

Wait a minute. What was he worried about? Hayden would say no. In spite of the *#hottie* in her tweet, she would never agree to an engagement to him. What was a few days—worse case, a few weeks—in jail to a tabloid darling like her? She'd be released early due to overcrowding, and then she'd turn the experience into a new reality show, maybe a book.

He could say yes and not piss off the old man. "I'll do it."

"I knew you would do the right thing." Middleton leaned over and stuck out his hand. "Welcome to the family."

Liam reached out and shook it, while he silently prayed that Hayden wouldn't stray from her MO. Everything hinged on her saying no. An engagement, even a fake one, to Hayden would test his character, and he feared he'd fail it. The volatile chemistry between them promised too many pleasures... not an option for a guy who vowed to abstain from sex until he married. Never mind jail, Liam would be headed straight for hell.

Chapter 5

Hayden hated being summoned to her father's office like a naughty child sent to the principal. Always reprimands and never—*Good job, Hayden. Profits from the candied nuts sector have tripled since you've taken over.* Never—*I'm proud of you for organizing the corporate charity ball.*

Why hadn't she quit years ago? A multimillionaire from her own company, she didn't need her father's money, nor had she even touched the trust fund her *grand-mère* had bequeathed to her. Hayden liked to be independent of her father's whims.

But she also held on to the stubborn belief that the legacy of Middleton Nuts should be passed down to her instead of her damn, perfect half brother. Perfect in the eyes of her father anyway.

It wasn't that she didn't love Harry—everyone did. But it irked her that her father treated her younger, illegitimate brother like the prince of the Middleton empire. Hayden was far more business savvy, and while Harry had a knack for seeming to stay out of trouble, Hayden knew better. She often came to her brother's rescue, whether it was taking the blame for something minor or adding an arrest to her already long record.

At least this morning she'd managed to handle the detectives with no problem.

31

She hoped last night wouldn't get Liam in trouble with the Cougars. Doubtful, considering he'd already been announced as the starting QB. Her father wouldn't jeopardize the season by firing or suspending a key player. Besides, Liam had saved her at the club.

Heat spread through her body at the memory of his firm hand on her butt as he hauled her to his car, and then later the feel of his breath mingling with hers, and the way his light brown eyes darkened with lust when he looked at her mouth. A saint in his actions, but a sinner lay behind that handsome face. What would it take to make him snap? To shed the façade? To make him fuck her silly?

Now, where had that thought come from? She didn't even like him. *Well, maybe a little.*

Shaking off thoughts of him, she turned on her tablet to attend to her own empire. She reviewed the campaign ad for the new perfume she was launching in a few weeks. The type font didn't look quite right, so she shot off an e-mail to her assistant. Engrossed in her own work, she ignored the annoying buzz that sounded at the secretary's desk.

"Ms. Middleton, your father will see you now."

"Thank you." She smiled at his new secretary. Was her father banging the bombshell after hours? Hayden kept tapping away. Her father had left her waiting outside his office for almost an hour. Two could play at this game.

Moments later her father bellowed, "Hayden, get in here now."

She hit the send button again before sweeping into the office. "Sorry, Daddy." She waved the tablet in the air. "Business before family. Just like you always say."

"I never said that," he said through clenched teeth.

"Actions speak louder than words." How she preened with pride over that comeback. Her father might preach about the importance of family, but business came first.

"It appears Judge Mayer agrees."

As intended, the retort wiped the smile right off her face. Panic fluttered in her stomach.

"Sit." Her father jabbed a finger at a chair. "The judge isn't pleased about your little escapade at Martini Madness last night."

As her brain scrambled for a return volley, she eased into the leather chair in front of his desk. "I'm sure a campaign contribution from you will put him in a better mood." The recovery would have been clever, except for the slight tremor in her voice.

Her father didn't miss a beat. "It's nice to have friends in high places. But not this time. The judge spoke of revoking your probation."

The flutter of panic morphed into a brick. "But I didn't do anything."

"That thug you call a friend fired a gun." He pounded a fist on the desk. "A gun, Hayden! You could've been killed."

"Daddy, let's not be dramatic." She didn't mention that Franco was actually Harry's friend.

"Me? This coming from the queen of drama?"

"That drama has made me rich. You know my sales spike when I'm in the news."

"I'm tired of this argument, Hayden. So is Judge May-er."

"So I'm going to jail? That's it? There's nothing I can do? PSA? Community service?" Her voice rose with each word. "I'll do anything."

Her father folded his hands, expression smug. "That's what I was hoping to hear." He paused. "So how much do you like Liam McQueen?"

"As this year's starting quarterback, you mean?" She played dumb, as if she didn't know the abrupt change in subject was about last night.

"No, as your new fiancé."

Hayden thought she had braced herself for whatever her father threw at her. But this? He'd done the impossible. He'd rendered her speechless.

He lit a cigar and took a big puff. "When the judge heard you and Liam were announcing your engagement today, he'd agreed not to revoke your probation. I explained that you two were out celebrating last night."

"You lied to the judge?"

"I wasn't lying."

"Have you gone completely senile? Should I call a nursing home?"

Her father leveled a hard gaze at her across the desk. "You should be thanking me. I saved your ass. Judge Mayer is a big fan of McQueen's. He even offered to preside over your wedding ceremony."

Hayden's eyes widened until she thought they'd pop right out of her skull and roll onto the carpet. "I am not marrying Liam McQueen."

"You spent the night at his place."

Hayden laughed. "Is that what this is all about? It's not 1950, Daddy."

"Judge Mayer is old-fashioned."

"Well, so is Liam." She cut the air with her hands.

"Nothing happened."

"Which is why I trust McQueen to be your pretend fiancé."

"Pretend?"

"I set the wedding date for after the Championship." He leaned forward and with a meaningful look, he whispered. "And after your probation ends."

Hayden paused. *Hmmm. No. No.* What was she thinking? "Liam will never agree to it."

"He already has."

Anger and confusion warred inside her. For now, confusion won out. Why would Liam lie for her? Money? No, he had money. Not as much as her family did, but still Liam wasn't the type to take a bribe. Had her father threatened Liam with some scandal? Threatened to take away the starting QB position? The Middletons could be ruthless, underhanded bastards. "What did you do?"

"Nothing."

"Dad...*dy*?" She drew out his name in accusation.

"He didn't want to see you go to jail."

"And...?" She knew there was more. Liam may be a nice guy, but no one was *that* nice.

"He owes me."

"You guilted him into it?" Hayden squeezed her eyes shut as she felt heat flame in her cheeks. How could she ever face Liam? First he'd rejected her last night and now this. She stiffened her back and took a deep breath. "Fine, I'll go to jail. Hell, if Martha Stewart can do time, so can I." The claim came out with more bravado than she felt.

"You will do no such thing. No daughter of mine is going to jail. The Middleton name will not be tarnished."

She folded her arms. "Way too late for that."

"Hayden, if you don't do this, I'm writing you out of my will."

"I don't need your precious money. I have plenty of money of my own."

"Not if I sue for conservatorship. I'll run your business and control every cent of your funds. You'll need me to approve your every move.

"I'll fight you." Though at the moment she had no fight in her. The contents of her stomach threatened to spew over his desk.

"And you'll lose."

She worried he might be right. She resorted to begging. "Daddy, please—"

"Hayden, spare me the wide blue eyes."

She brought out the big guns. Her father had always hated to see her cry. With the cigar smoke filtering through the air, it was easy to make the tears flow. She added a sniff for effect. When he walked around his desk to pat her on the back, she controlled the urge to smile. She'd won.

"It's for your own good, Hayden." He handed her a tissue from his desk. "Now dry those crocodile tears."

Wait. *What?* In frustration, she snatched the tissue. "What about Liam? Aren't you worried I'll corrupt your quarterback? The press will have a field day. I'm no good, remember?"

"Then be better."

Ha! Hayden had avoided prison like a criminal Houdini. This time would be no different. She was going to do everything in her power to force Liam to break the engagement. She'd find all his buttons and push each one.

But for now she'd go along with this farce and get what belonged to her. "I'll do it on one condition. According to the terms of *Grand-Mère's* will, I'm now entitled to her engagement ring."

"For a real engagement, not this."

"A technicality. Ring or no deal."

Her father released a sigh of resignation. "I'll go to the bank tomorrow with your future husband."

Future husband? She scoffed. "You mean pretend future husband."

"Of course."

Their engagement wouldn't last the week. With his holier-than-thou beliefs, Liam would be running in the other direction before the next game.

And she already knew the perfect offense play. *Sex.*

Chapter 6

After speaking with Hayden, the doorman pointed Liam to her building's bank of elevators. Ten minutes later, he still stood frozen in front of her penthouse door. The ring in his pocket felt like a fifty-pound barbell.

He had seriously misjudged her willingness to go to jail. Her father said she was terrified, but too proud to admit it. Liam had his doubts. Hayden seemed fearless.

Perhaps she thought she could walk all over Liam with those sexy stilettos for the next few months? Pretend they were engaged but still do whatever she wanted with whatever guy she pleased. *Not in this lifetime.*

He pounded on her door. He would make it clear from the start that he expected her to behave. But the instant she opened the door, he realized he might be the one who'd have trouble behaving.

"You're late, Liam. I was getting worried."

His heart halted mid-beat. Her dress appeared to be created from liquid gold. The fabric draped across her body, hugging every luscious curve. The hue enhanced the glow of her tanned skin. As she smiled at him, he willed his heart to stop pounding.

"Don't you think that dress is a little tight?" he asked through a clenched jaw.

The mischievous light shining in her eyes dulled for a

moment. "I've put on a few pounds since I bought it. I'll skip dessert tonight."

"That's not what I meant." *Darn.* Had he hurt her with his unthinking remark? "You look hot. Too hot."

She tilted her chin with every bit of sass that was Hayden. "Maybe we should skip dinner and I could change into something more naughty. Would you like to help?" She turned on her heel.

Sighing, Liam followed her inside.

"You know," she continued, "you can still change your mind about the engagement."

"More like come to my senses," he mumbled.

"I heard that."

"You were meant to." At this point, what was one more lie? "You redecorated," he added without thinking. Expecting to see a nightmare of pink leopard furniture and white shag carpeting, he was shocked at the sophisticated palate of silver and light blues. Did she change the bedroom too? His cock itched to find out if the ceiling mirror remained.

Hayden arched an eyebrow. "Why Liam, were you a fan of *Hayden's Place?*"

Crap. Watching it had been his guilty pleasure, but he played it off by saying, "Who hasn't seen an episode or two."

"And you still want to help me? Aren't you worried I'll tarnish your saintly image?"

"Want to?" He shrugged. "More like have to." The more he thought about it, the less he liked the idea of her in jail.

"Whatever." Hayden looked down at her perfectly

manicured nails. "Well, do you have it?"

Liam knew exactly what *it* was, but decided to have a little fun. "Have what?"

Putting her hands on her hips, she said, "The ring, you idiot."

He reached into his pocket for the obscenely large, pink diamond ring. Stroking the case, he said, "You mean, my precious."

"Dork."

"You didn't like *The Lord of the Rings*? That's grounds for annulment."

"An annulment requires a wedding first. That's never happening with us." She tried to snatch the case, but he slapped her hand away. "Hey, give it."

He raised the ring box up in the air.

"Liam!" She attempted to pull his arm down. When that failed, she jumped several times trying to reach it. Quite impressive with those five-inch heels.

"Liam! Come on! It belonged to my *grand-mère*."

Feeling like a jerk, he relented and handed over her family heirloom.

She opened the case with a reverence that went beyond greed. Her eyes softened, and for a moment, he thought she might cry. Suddenly, he wanted to know more about Hayden and what made her tick. "Were you close?"

"Very. My grandparents were married sixty years. They died within two months of each other." She looked up at him. "Like one couldn't live without the other."

Guilt licked at his conscience. Their fake engagement was making a mockery of the sacred vows of husband and wife. "The diamond is huge."

"The size of the rock means nothing to me. The person who wore it meant everything."

For once, he didn't detect a hint of her usual sarcasm. "How poetic of you, Hayden. I almost feel like I should drop down on one knee."

Hayden made a face. "Spare me a fake proposal."

"As long as you act like the engagement is real." He stepped closer. "You may even have to kiss me."

She tilted her head, giving him that Jessica Rabbit look. "It will be a chore, but I suppose it's the least I can do, considering you're saving me from jail."

"The least you can do?" he scoffed. "You're going to regret those words."

"Oh no, I do believe you'll be the one full of regret." She handed him back the case. "I changed my mind." She stuck out her left hand and wiggled her fingers. "Down on your knees, Liam. I'd like that proposal now."

Hayden was a piece of work. If she thought he'd kneel at her feet, she had seriously misjudged him.

"Catch!" Smiling, he tossed the ring case high and away.

"Liam!" Without missing a beat, she dove over the top of the couch. Like a pro, she made a one-handed reception as she landed face down on the cushions.

"Nice," he said more about her ass than the catch. "Now, let's get to dinner. It's time the public got a look at the happy couple."

"You can order a glass of wine," he said after the waiter left with their orders. He hated when people treated his sobriety like an egg ready to crack. He was responsible for his decisions, for his actions. Life was full of choices. And tonight the only temptation was Hayden's cleavage. He thought he was doing an admirable job of keeping his eyes level with hers.

"I can't. It's part of my probation." Hayden played with her dangling earring as she spoke.

Was it a habit of hers? Or was she flashing the engagement ring to the whole restaurant? Their charade had been covered in all the gossip columns today, and they were drawing stares, which was saying something in a room full of people like these. The rich and famous dined at ultra-exclusive LeFarge to avoid being bothered for autographs. Liam disliked being disturbed while eating too, but he never refused a fan.

Dinner passed amicably. Good food, and he had to admit good company. Hayden's wit kept him on his toes. Her attempts to shock him amused him, but he had her number.

"That was delicious," he said after he finished his meal of salmon and steamed vegetables. "During the season, I don't eat out much. I'm pretty good in the kitchen. My mother taught me how to cook."

"I can't cook." Her shoeless foot ran along his calf. "My skills are more about the bedroom."

Liam reached under the table as she reached his thigh. Massaging her foot, he grinned. "I'm pretty good there too."

Her eyes widened for a split second, but then narrowed as she yanked her foot away. "Liam, I think you are all teeth and no bite."

"It's all about the tongue," he shot back.

Hayden wiggled in her chair. Before she could respond, the waiter delivered her cheesecake and coffee for the both of them. Liam liked a woman who ordered dessert, but he loved how Hayden enjoyed it, like a woman in the throes of an orgasm. Was she doing it on purpose to drive him out of his mind? Instead of taking a sip of coffee, he reached for the glass of water and took a long drink.

"Hayden, take pity on me."

"What? Is this turning you on?" Seemingly innocent blue eyes didn't match the naughty tone in her voice.

"I haven't had sex in two years. A light breeze turns me on."

"Good to know." She sensuously licked a spoonful of cheesecake. "Oh yeah." Then taking another spoonful, she placed it in her mouth and sucked. "Mmmmm... soooo... good."

Liam shifted in his seat, trying to broker some room in his pants for his erection. He'd give anything to be that spoon. Anything. Except his soul. He'd made a vow he wouldn't have sex again until he got married. After two years of celibacy, one evening with Hayden should have been a piece of cake.

Cake? Cheesecake. He shut his eyes, but he couldn't shut his ears, which made it so much worse. With the tiny moans escaping her lips, he imagined her licking his cock. Sucking on it. Swallowing it.

"Good to the last drop." The click of the spoon on the clean plate sounded the end of his torture.

It was going to be a long five month fake engagement. Hayden may be on probation but Liam felt like the one sentenced to jail.

After he paid the check and they stepped outside, he realized the crowd of paparazzi had tripled since they arrived. He'd warned her father about this. Liam didn't want to spend hours answering questions about his personal life.

"Will your engagement affect the season?" yelled one of the paparazzi. "Is it a publicity stunt?"

Good question. Liam wouldn't put it past the old man. Where did Middleton think Hayden inherited her love of the spotlight? Had her father leaked the newly engaged couple's whereabouts? Had Hayden?

As the shouting photographers jostled for a better angle, Liam took her small hand and scanned the sidewalk, plotting their escape route like he would a play on the field. He could use a few of his linemen about now. He bulldozed a path to the curb, using his strength and height, keeping Hayden close behind him.

Arriving at his Hummer, he glanced over his shoulder. Her self-satisfied smile confirmed his suspicion. He itched to kiss that bratty grin off her face. *Okay.* If she wanted to give people something to talk about, he'd oblige.

He whirled her into his arms ready to scratch his annoyance away. Once their lips met in a heated clash, he realized it wasn't an itch at all, but an unquenchable thirst for the taste of her and a raving hunger to feed upon her breath. Hayden was his decadent dessert. She tasted like sin and spice and nothing nice.

He ran his hands down her curves. Reaching her ass, he pulled her closer, hoping the softness of her belly would relieve the ache in his cock. Instead, he hardened to the point of frustration.

God bless the press. They were the only reason he wouldn't toss Hayden into the backseat and have his wicked way with her.

He wished he wasn't giving the photographers such a nice shot. He could already see tomorrow's front page. *The Cougars' star quarterback cradling something besides a football in his hands—Hayden Middleton's booty.*

That didn't stop him from deepening the kiss as the flashes went off.

Chapter 7

O h. Dear. God. Liam knew how to kiss.

Kiss? What an inadequate word to describe the tender assault.

Every nerve ending of Hayden's skin pricked alive, every fragment of her being hummed with awakening. All. From. A. Kiss.

She felt his hard-on press against her belly. The size promised fulfillment in every way. So did his tongue. Liam kissed her like he owned her. Controlled her. Mastered her. With her mind numb, her body rendered weak, a heavy weight of desire pressed down on her chest. She thought her heart had ceased to beat. She slid a hand up to thread through his reddish-brown waves. Melting into him, she sighed the last bit of air from her lungs. For a moment she depended on him to keep her upright and for the very air she breathed.

Then he broke away. She gasped, her lifeline ripped from her.

Opening the passenger door, he said, "Get in."

Startled, she breathed on her own again, but remained unable to move. He tapped her ass, nodded to the Hummer, and then hoisted her inside. More flashes from the cameras caught the action frame by frame. For once she didn't care about publicity. She didn't dare look into the lens—afraid what the photos might reveal. A blush? Dreamy eyes?

She looked anxiously to the driver's seat, waiting for Liam to slide in. Then what? She'd been on the receiving end of sloppy smooches, halfhearted pecks, and rushed kisses that only meant to lead to the main event. But Liam's? She could live off his kisses. Or die from them. If one kiss from him could create this much havoc in her, then what would more do?

She'd warned her father she'd be a bad influence on his star player. The PDA was so out of character for Liam's revamped Christian image. Apparently, her making out with a spoonful of cheesecake had pushed the choirboy over the edge.

But instead of reveling in her success, a twinge of unease fought with her normal devil-may-care attitude. Liam started the car. "I think they bought it."

What? Had he only kissed her senseless to prove to the paparazzi that the engagement was real? Anger rose in her blood, but in truth she was more hurt than mad.

He looked to her, seemingly unconcerned about the paparazzi mobbing the vehicle. "I hope that wasn't too much of a chore for you?"

How clever of him to throw her earlier dig back at her. But that's not what annoyed her. That he didn't appear the least bit affected by the kiss did. "So what if you're a great kisser. It means nothing." Damn, she meant to say *good*, not *great*.

"It means everything, Hayden." His gaze dropped to her lap. "Everything."

Dear God, she was ready to drop her panties. Well, if

she were wearing any, that is.

"Speechless?" Liam laughed. "Score one for me."

It wasn't fair. Not only was her plan to drive him away not working, but Liam gave back as good as he got. And he seemed to be enjoying that way more than he did kissing her.

She fumed as he inched the tank like vehicle through the horde of frenzied paparazzi.

"And Hayden. Don't ever pull a stunt like that again."

"What stunt?" It was too dark to waste an innocent flash of her baby blues. She'd play that trick later when it counted for something bigger.

He threw her a sideways glance. "Really?"

She thought about denying that she had alerted her media contacts, but why lie about it? If he realized his life would be a media circus, then maybe he would break the engagement before something more vulnerable was broken—like her heart. She could see herself easily falling in love with him. But she wasn't about to change who she was for him or any man. "I'll do whatever I want with the press. Get used to it."

He pulled away from the crowd and sped down the street away from the pursuit of several cars. "I was talking about dessert. Don't tease me like that again."

Oh. An awkward silence enveloped them. Awkward for Hayden, anyway. She loved to be the center of attention, the total opposite of Liam. How would they ever make anyone believe he liked her, much less that he wanted to marry her? *That's the whole point of this outing, isn't it? To prove to Liam that a fake engagement won't work?*

When he pulled up to the curb in front of her building,

she tugged on the sleeve of his suit jacket. "You don't have to walk me up."

"Yes, I do." Liam nodded toward the two photographers unsuccessfully hiding behind the large planters by the entrance. While the doorman struggled to hold them back, he slipped his hands around her waist and lifted her out of the large vehicle.

Their gazes met. His eyes heated into molten pools of amber. All the noise of the city faded away. She smiled, realizing he wasn't as unaffected as he pretended. He slid her body against his as he slowly put her down. Would he kiss her again?

A photographer lunged, jostling the car door, ruining the moment. Liam pushed the offender to the ground and rushed her inside the building. The silence continued in the elevator. Was he mad at her?

"Coming in?" She opened the door to her apartment. If he was going to be mad, she might as well make it count.

"No."

"We're engaged." Her fingers danced up his chest. "No reason why we can't have a little fun."

"Fake engaged. I made a vow."

"Don't tell me you're one of those born-again virgins?"

"A virgin?" Liam laughed. "Don't worry, Hayden. When it comes to a wedding night, my future wife will be getting all the benefits of all my past experience." He pressed her hand flat against his heart. "Too bad you aren't her."

She slid her hand up to tighten his tie until she nearly strangled him. "Fine. I'll just use my vibrator."

With a smile, he loosened the knot, exposing the muscular cords of his neck. "But you'll be thinking of me."

Damn. She would be thinking of him. She'd relive that epic kiss and fantasize about the rest. The way he'd leisurely lick her body, his tongue playing with her tingling clit, the feel of his cock pushing inside her. Caught up in the vision, she didn't notice his retreating back.

"Liam! Not even a kiss goodnight?" she pouted.

He turned, his arms open and palms up. "Why bother? There are no cameras around for you to play up to."

"Hey, you're the one who kissed me," she shouted down the hall. She winced, hoping none of the neighbors were disturbed by the commotion. Hayden was on probation for that too. One more incident and the co-op board would live up to its threat to force the sale of her penthouse.

Liam poked his head out the elevator doors. "Hey Hayden." He blew her kiss. "Catch."

She fisted her hands and stomped her foot. How dare he remind her of his non-proposal! She slammed the door. To hell with her neighbors. And to hell with Liam McQueen.

Chapter 8

As the team owner's daughter, the first game of the season was always a little nerve-wracking for Hayden. But as the quarterback's fiancée, the stakes were even higher. At least it got her back into her father's good graces. After her last arrest, he had banned her from the stadium.

Hannah Hahn and Angel Burner lounged in the owner's box as usual, while the other wives and girlfriends sat in a reserved area outside. Preferential treatment was given to the supermodel and her friend, neither of whom liked Hayden.

Technically she was one of them now. Hayden, however, had never been very nice to the wives or girlfriends of the players.

But she needed to make nice now.

Last year, Samantha Jameson would've made the twosome a trio. Her husband, Ryan Terell, had retired at the end of last season. Hayden knew what the public didn't. Headaches had sidelined the tight end, not his aging knees. The doctors warned the veteran player that another hit to the head could possibly end more than his career. Hayden wondered how he was handling retirement.

Perhaps this was a way to break the ice with the two wives.

Hayden stalled for a moment but knew that she needed

to make the effort. She stepped down and took a seat across the aisle. After saying hello and receiving no response, she asked, "How are Samantha and Ryan?"

Hannah didn't look over. "They're fine."

Not promising. It felt like the temperature in the room dropped fifty degrees, as though they were sitting outside in the middle of winter instead of watching from a climate-controlled room in the beginning of September.

"And how's Gabby, Angel?" Hayden bit her lip, not sure how her query about Angel's young daughter would be received. Out of all of the wives, she'd given Billy's wife the hardest time. But who wouldn't be dubious of a woman who out of the blue slapped a paternity suit on a professional football player?

"She's fine."

Apparently Angel was taking Hannah's lead. "Look, I'm sorry I was such a bitch to you last season."

Angel looked to Hannah who shrugged.

"I'm sorry I ran out of your wedding. Liam was being such a jerk." Hayden had represented the Middleton family at Billy and Angel's wedding. "Did you know he smacked my ass, damn hard, then pushed me out onto the dance floor?"

"Just in time for my bouquet to hit you square in the head." Angel giggled.

Hannah joined in. "I must've viewed that clip on YouTube a hundred times."

"The whole world did." For the first time since the incident, Hayden laughed about it.

"Is that when your secret love affair started?" asked Angel.

Secret love affair? Before the night at Martini Madness, she'd run into Liam since the wedding, but he'd always been the same disapproving pain in the ass he'd always been. *Hmmm.* Kind of like the adult version of a little boy pulling a little girl's ponytail on the playground. Did Liam like her? She laughed, shaking her head with the realization. "Yeah, I guess it did."

Not wanting to dwell on the crazy idea that Liam had feelings for her, she plucked two small paper bags from the counter. She was eager to change the subject. "Have you tried the Cougar Jax yet? It's a new recipe that I'm thinking of adding to the candied nuts division."

"I can't. Carbs." Hannah held up her hands as if the mere sight would add a pound or two to her svelte frame.

Angel grabbed a bag. "Yeah, but I can."

"Who's the bitch now?" joked Hannah.

The three women laughed like they were old friends.

"Now let's see that ring," Hannah said.

The request was music to a girl's ear. Hayden stuck out her hand and they ooo-ed and ah-ed over the size, color, and art-deco setting. She almost felt like one of them, but she really wasn't, was she? Their husbands loved them. Married them because of that love. Hayden's engagement wasn't real. She doubted she'd ever be married like them. Or loved.

Perhaps if she were more like them, Liam might fall for her too. Maybe if she lost twenty pounds? Maybe if she kept her opinions to herself? Maybe if she developed an ounce of maternal instinct? Maybe if she read the Bible?

Stop it! The last thought was too close for comfort. She was enough. She was more than enough. She didn't want

Liam to want her. *Well, maybe a little.* Maybe more than a little.

As the game progressed, the owner's box grew silent. The score—0 to 7—favored the away team. The Cougars looked flat and Liam's aim off. They'd had a perfect preseason and had home-field advantage, but the Warriors were pounding the Cougars' offense. She gripped her seat each time Liam was sacked. Normally, she'd be screaming from her seat for the quarterback to scramble, but she couldn't do that now. It wouldn't do for Liam's fiancée to lose her cool in front of her father's guests.

Only seconds remained on the clock as Liam threw an impossible pass. The opposing cornerback beat out Billy Burner to catch it in the end zone. Interception. Game over. A loss for the Cougars—and Liam.

"See you at the next home game." Angel grabbed another bag of nuts on her way up the steps, apparently unconcerned that *her* husband had missed the pass.

Hayden nodded, biting her tongue.

Hannah followed Angel without a word but then stopped and came back down the steps. "Hayden, a word of advice."

"Sure."

"Be Liam's fiancée, not the owner's daughter. The players get enough grief from the coaches, press, and fans. Your man needs your support."

"I'll break out the pom-poms." She'd shore up his ego for the sake of next week's game. She knew her football in and out, but she'd play dumb and pretend he didn't stink up the field today.

Just a week ago, she would have called him a loser to

his face, but now she couldn't bring herself to do it. His poor play was partly her fault with all the media coverage leading up to the game. She'd done enough damage.

Besides, she had a part to play—the adoring fiancée. Unfortunately, it was becoming less and less of an act.

Chapter 9

While Liam iced his shoulder in the trainer's' room, the team's cute but no nonsense public relations liaison kept the press at bay. Thank God for Meredith. Faced with a no-win scenario, Liam didn't know which he dreaded more—tackling the sportswriters or Hayden, who he was sure would have a lot to say.

He didn't need his quarterback rating to tell him he'd played his worst game as a Cougar—or ever—which was saying something since he'd had a lot of bad games as a professional quarterback.

Today, he couldn't hit the side of the barn he'd use for practice as a kid. The quarterback was the pulse of the offense and Liam's arm was dead on arrival. Throw after throw, too hard, too soft, too high, or too low. Getting sacked three times didn't help. His body ached from the blunt force of the tackles, but nothing hurt as much as losing did.

Near the end of the final quarter, he'd thought the only good thing the analysts might say is that he hadn't thrown an interception. But he jinxed himself even thinking about that. Not that he really believed in jinxes, but the thought rattled his confidence on the last play.

He didn't need to see a replay on ESPN to remember how he lost the first game of the season.

Billy Burner ran from the sideline to join them in the huddle. "Hail Mary the ball to me."

Liam hated the stupid nickname for the desperation move. Long pass in the final seconds, low probability of success. The quarterback who originated the term said he'd need to pray for divine intervention to connect with his receiver.

"Right up your alley, McQueen," Hondo had said.

Liam ignored him. Just as he didn't believe in the jinx, he didn't believe that God cared much about football. Miracles belonged to the dying, not to millionaire athletes. Liam never prayed to the win the game. He did pray for God to make him strong and to keep him and the players free from injury. "Just keep Dunham off my ass."

The huddle broke and Liam read the defense as he approached the line of scrimmage. *Blitz.* They were going to come at him. He could call an audible to try and throw them off, but the defense, heck, the whole stadium knew there was only one play, one chance for the home team to tie the game. Instead he decided to throw them off with a quick count. He backed off into the shotgun position. "Code red one," he'd yelled.

Hondo knew the signal and hiked the ball back to Liam's waiting hands. His linemen bought him precious seconds as Burner flew down the field, but Liam needed more time as Dunham broke through and chased him out of the pocket. Hurdling over a fallen lineman, he released the ball just before hitting the line of scrimmage. The crowd roared as the ball sailed in a movie-perfect arc toward the end zone. Then the ball brushed off Burner's fingertips and landed into the Warriors cornerback's hands.

Intercepted. Game over.

The collective moan from the fans had deafened Liam's ears more than any cheer ever had. He'd disappointed them. Again. Then the booing rained down from the stands. Some players claimed they couldn't hear the fans, but Liam felt each hiss and catcall like a tackle from a charging lineman.

"Sorry man," Burner said as they'd headed to the locker room.

"No, bro, it's all on me." Liam thumped his chest.

"Win as a team, lose as a team."

Liam nodded, even though he knew it wasn't true. Nothing would be said, but his teammates would silently place the blame on him, especially the defense who held the Warriors to only a single touchdown, keeping the Cougars in the game. Then there was Romer, the rookie quarterback, who would no doubt be gloating about his rival's bad start.

So Liam iced his shoulder and took his time in the shower, going over in his head how he should handle the inevitable onslaught of questions.

Dressed in a suit and feeling calmer, he left the safe haven of the trainers' room ready to face off against the press. Because of the media frenzy created by his engagement, the Cougars had set up a formal press conference rather than the usual post-game stand-up.

At least a table would separate him and the press. Win or lose, he hated how the reporters got up in his face with their microphones and cameras after every game. He almost felt sorry for Hayden, dealing with media on a daily basis. Though she seemed to enjoy all the attention.

As he took his seat, flashes from the cameras nearly blinded him, and the shouts of a dozen reporters muddled his ability to distinguish a specific question. But he caught old man Middleton's glare from the back of the room. Good, maybe the owner was having second thoughts about the wisdom of using Liam as his sacrificial lamb.

Determined to set the tone of the conference, Liam leaned forward to the microphone to issue a statement. "I'm not talking about my personal life."

Meredith, handling her public relations' role, pointed to a reporter from the *New Jersey Examiner*. "Tony, get us started."

"How much do you think your poor play has to do with your engagement to the daughter of the Cougars owner?" the reporter asked.

Liam rubbed the tension knotting the back of his neck. Maybe he could deflect further inquiry with a self-effacing remark. "I don't need anyone's help to suck. Just look at last year's Championship." That earned him a few chuckles.

Tony followed up. "So you don't think Hayden Middleton is a distraction?"

"During a game?" Liam decided to stick with humor. "Only if she came running naked out on the field. Did I miss that too?"

A burst of laughter sounded off the walls. Liam joined in. "Now can we talk about football? Otherwise, I'm out of here."

"Given your past, isn't your engagement to a known party girl a danger to your sobriety?" The question came from the back on the room.

Scowling, Liam identified a reporter named Ender—a

hack who had gleefully written about his hard fall from grace. Who let that prick in? The team had revoked Ender's press privileges long before Liam even joined the team, after the so-called sports reporter targeted running back Miller and his supermodel wife with a torrid personal piece that had nothing to do with the game.

Liam didn't intend for the same thing to happen to Hayden and him.

"I said no questions about my personal life." Before anger got the best of him, he rose from his seat and headed deliberately away from the microphone.

The room exploded into chaos as he walked out the door. Meredith followed him, her heels clacking like cleats on the concrete floor, pleading with him to return to the lion's den. He kept walking. Middleton created the media circus; he could darn well rein in the rabid reporters too. The sour smell of stale beer hit his senses as he passed by the entrance to the stands. Even though beer wasn't his poison on choice, a craving for a drink hit him hard.

And it had nothing to with Hayden. She might he harder on him than the press, but at least she'd stick to football, even if it was to tell him he sucked. That he could handle. Questions about his past left him ashamed. He'd yet to forgive himself and he never would.

He didn't expect to find his fake fiancée waiting with the wives and girlfriends. But there she was, chatting with Hannah and Angel. Now there was a turn of events. He'd heard first hand how nasty Hayden was to Angel last season. Now they were laughing like best friends.

She waved good-bye and walked over to him with a big fake smile plastered across her face. It was a little creepy.

Running back and confronting the reporters seemed less scary.

"Hey, babe," she said as she reached up to pat his shoulder.

"Hey," he said cautiously. Where was the Hayden that called him a loser? Who hated the use of the word, hey?"

They walked to his car. "It's only the first game of the season. You'll get em' next week."

"Yeah." Confused, he slowed up as they reached his Hummer.

Hayden kept on to the passenger side. She turned to face him. "And don't get me started on the refs."

"Okay, did you have a brain hemorrhage or something?"

"What? I'm just trying to be a good fiancée."

Suddenly, he didn't care about the false engagement. He pulled her into his arms. "Then, I guess I should be a good fiancé and kiss you."

"Like, finally."

A soft mewing sound escaped her mouth as he brushed his lips against hers. The desire to bring out the feline side of her hit him hard. He wanted her to hiss with frustration when he wouldn't let her come, to roar with release when he did, and then purr her satisfaction as she fell asleep in his arms.

But they had an audience. He let her go and nodded to the crowded parking garage. "We have spectators."

She looked oddly disappointed. "Good to know."

Liam signed a couple of autographs for the kids who asked, glad that anyone valued his signature after that loss. A couple of Hayden's fans asked for her autograph too.

Once the crowd dispersed, they both slid into his car.

"Look Hayden, I appreciate the show of support, especially in public." He started the car and then turned her, outstretching his right arm across the passenger seat. "But you don't have to boost my ego. When we're alone, you can be real with me."

"Oh, thank God." She put his face between her hands. "Because you totally sucked today." Then she planted a big kiss on his lips.

The kiss she unleashed softened the blow of her words, but hardened him elsewhere.

He groaned when she climbed over the console to straddle his thighs. Grabbing her luscious ass, he pressed her against his erection. She rocked her body along his throbbing cock and tightened her thighs against his. The bruising pain from the beating of the defense and the humiliation of defeat faded until only one part of him ached.

She broke away, panting for breath. Her blue eyes darkened with lust. "You can score with me, Liam," she whispered.

"You're killing me, Hayden."

"That's the idea," she said her voice soft. He held her gaze as she sucked his thumb into her mouth.

To hell with his stupid vow of celibacy. She wanted him and he wanted her. *Now.* Losing himself in her would numb today's loss. She'd ease his need for a drink...

Then she pushed back her hair and he caught sight of her engagement ring—the diamond that had sanctified a marriage that had lasted sixty years.

No woman had ever tempted him like Hayden. Not

even close. But he didn't want to lose himself or be numb with her. Just the opposite. He wanted to feel with his whole heart, to find himself again.

Hayden was a beautiful distraction and a naughty influence. She wasn't a danger to his sobriety, but to his sanity. Heaven help him.

But it wasn't his heavenly Father who saved him from breaking his vow in the front seat of his Hummer.

Hayden's father pounded his fist on the hood. Hayden giggled as she untangled herself. Plopping back into the passenger seat, she zipped down the window. "Hello, Daddy."

The fury on her father's face made Liam thankful that she was protected in his tank.

"What the hell are you thinking?" Middleton said more to Hayden than to Liam.

"I was just consoling my fiancé about the game," she said with a toss of her head.

"You're going to be the death of me, Hayden."

Liam knew exactly how he felt.

Chapter 10

Hayden surveyed her father's decorated yacht with dread. She loved a good party, but the impromptu engagement soiree her father was throwing tonight—a black and white cocktail party—had her stomach in knots. The fake engagement was becoming all too real. So were her feelings for Liam.

Liam squeezed her hand. "Nervous?"

"No," she lied. She looked up at him, her heart stopping at the sparkle in his chocolate diamond eyes. They said diamonds are a girl's best friend, and Hayden did love her diamonds. That must explain why his eyes fascinated her so much. But she didn't want Liam as a best friend—she wanted the sexy quarterback as her lover.

And in truth, much more. Somehow, she had let him sneak into her heart.

She smoothed her white satin dress and linked her arm through his. Dressed in a black suit and white silk tie, he looked like a powerful CEO. His slicked-back hair, while chic, made her fingers itch to mess it up. The breeze off the river carried his scent of earth and mint. She wet her lips, longing for the cool freshness of his kisses.

"Hayden, if you don't stop looking at me like that, I'm going to throw you in the river to cool off."

Damn. He'd caught her staring.

"You wouldn't dare." She laughed it off and defaulted to her best defense. "Why don't we ditch this party and have one of our own?"

"I'm waiting for my wedding night." He swatted her on the butt. "Now, behave."

"You are obsessed with my ass."

"Hayden, the whole world is obsessed with your ass," he said as if stating a fact.

She laughed with her whole heart, something only Liam seemed to be able to accomplish. He was right, though. There were probably more photos out there of her going than coming.

They stepped onto the gangway. Why did she feel like she was walking the gangplank instead? It wasn't even going to be a large gathering. She'd texted a group of her old friends, but none had responded. Not surprising. Even before good-guy Liam entered her life, she hadn't heard much from them. Once she traded in her cocktail dresses for pajamas because of her probation, her friends had disappeared one by one. They'd either deserted her for the wilder parties around New York, or they just didn't care.

At the time she couldn't blame them. If she were honest, she would have done the same thing to them. Who wanted to go to the movies or to dinner, when they could choose a party or club instead?

Except Hayden had discovered she kind of liked quieter evenings. That night at Martini Madness had been her brother Harry's idea. Then, he hadn't shown up, and Franko had pulled a gun. Now, Liam was stuck with her until her probation ended.

"What's your judge doing here?" he asked as they entered the yacht's interior space. "Did your father invite him?"

"Well, I certainly didn't." Hayden eyed the imposing figure of Judge Mayer chatting with her father in the corner. Why were they both smiling at her? She almost snagged a glass of champagne from a passing tray to calm her nerves.

Out of the corner of her eye, she saw her mother. Why wasn't she in Paris? *Please, please, don't be drunk.* Hayden watched her approach, noting the purple cocktail dress. *Maybe the shade was dark enough to look black?* The dress hung loose on her mother's slender figure. A figure that Hayden had not inherited.

"Darling, how could you? A mother should be the first to know. First, your engagement and now a surprise wedding!"

Wedding? Surprise? WTF. "It's an engagement party, Mother. A black and white themed event."

"Shhh. White's just for you." Her mom put a finger to her mouth then gave a drunken wink. "Introduce me to this hunk of man."

"This is Liam McQueen."

"An honor to meet you." Liam inclined his head.

"Please call me Charlize." Her mother waved an empty glass of champagne in the air. "Finally someone is making an honest woman of my daughter. Twenty-eight, and this is her first engagement. I was beginning to despair."

Hayden rolled her eyes. "Mother—"

"Your daughter is nothing but honest." Liam took Hayden's hand and kissed it.

Her mother's drunken laughter sounded louder in the

near-empty space. Hayden wondered what Liam thought about her mother's behavior. With all the alcohol around, would he be tempted to join in?

"Hayden, we need to speak in my office." Her father interrupted. "McQueen, you too. Charlize, greet the guests as they arrive. They should be here soon. In the meantime, try to stay upright for once."

Hayden winced at her father's cruel words, but followed him to his study. Harry and her father's attorney stood off to the side. *What the hell was going on?*

"I'll get right to it." Her father moved behind his desk. "Your engagement is becoming a media nightmare. It's time to end it."

"We told you the press wouldn't leave us alone," Hayden chimed in. She should have cheered with relief. This was what she'd been working toward. But oddly, she didn't feel much like celebrating. Suddenly, being right felt very wrong.

But then her father patted Liam on the back. "Once you're married, I'm confident the speculation will quiet down. Judge Mayer will be performing the ceremony tonight."

Relief turned to panic, but before Hayden could utter a protest, Liam said. "He threatened her with jail again, didn't he?"

"I told you he loved his football. Last week's loss, the lawsuit the photographer filed against you for pushing him down outside Hayden's apartment, and now," Her father held up a tabloid, "Ender's article claiming your engagement is fake."

"I don't care what the judge says. I'm not getting married," yelled Hayden.

"Keep your voice down. Do you want the judge to hear you?" Her father nodded to the open door. He left Liam's side to face her. "You either say your vows tonight or you'll be saying them behind a jail cell."

She glanced down at her white dress and at Liam's dark suit. Her father had manipulated them both.

She couldn't even look at Liam. "So I go to jail for a few weeks. Big deal."

"Five years," her father said flatly. "The judge thinks you tried to deceive the court. I assured him he was incorrect. Being a judge, he wanted proof. You'll marry Liam tonight or receive the maximum sentence."

Five years. Tears threatened, but she would not cry for real in front of anyone. She plopped in the nearest chair, defeated.

Liam stood toe to toe with her father, as if he were taking on the defensive line of an opposing team by himself. "I won't get married without my mother here."

"She'll be arriving shortly," her father told him. "I sent my plane for her earlier today."

"You were pretty sure of yourself, weren't you?" Liam asked calmly.

"I was sure of you, son."

Hayden couldn't believe the two of them. They were talking as if she wasn't there. As if she had no say in any of this. "You don't have to do this, Liam."

Shrugging, he smiled at her. "I'm not going to let you go to jail."

Her father cleared his throat. "First, there is the little matter of the pre-nup."

Liam didn't flinch continuing to hold her gaze.

She mouthed, "I'm sorry."

"It's a basic pre-nup," her father continued. "You keep what you have, she keeps what she has. Your finances are to remain separate. No marital assets. When you divorce, McQueen, you'll walk away with five million."

She wished she had drunk the glass of champagne to take away the sting of it all. She didn't know why she was surprised. This wasn't a love match—it was a business deal. "Only five? I'd hold out for ten, Liam."

"This isn't a football contract." Her father pounded a fist on the desk.

"You just made it one," Liam said back with just as much force. She bit her lip as he reviewed the pages. "I'll sign it, but first I want the judge to agree to lift Hayden's probation. I won't have the threat of jail hanging over her head." He threw the contract onto the desk. "Or mine."

Hayden's eyes widened. She'd never seen anything so sexy in her life. Was it because of the way he stood up to her father?

"The judge won't agree to it."

"Yes, I will," said Judge Mayer from the door. "I was already planning on it." He walked in pulling a document from his suit jacket and handed it to a shocked Hayden. "A wedding present."

"Thank you, Judge Mayer," her father said.

"My pleasure." He pulled out another piece of paper. "Of course, let's not forget the marriage license."

Another favor her father would owe to the judge. Hayden's hand shook as she signed it, but she noticed Liam's hand didn't. What was he thinking? Why wasn't he jumping ship?

"That leaves the pre-nup," said the lawyer, handing it to Liam.

Hayden held her breath.

Liam scratched out the five million dollar figure and wrote $0.00, initialed the change, and then signed on the dotted line. "I don't want your daughter's money."

She couldn't believe Liam did that for her. Tears sprung to her eyes.

"Idiot," said her brother.

"Harry!" Hayden shot him a look, but she wouldn't let him ruin this moment.

That Liam stood up to her father made her believe that maybe one day she could too. Her heart swelled with pride for the man she was about to marry. And perhaps it swelled with love too. Oh God, she was in love with her shotgun-husband-to-be.

"Now I'd like to have a moment alone with my bride."

To see her father rendered speechless would've been worth the five million dollars, but to see him dismissed was so much more than that. It was priceless.

Chapter 11

Liam craved a Scotch on the rocks like a dying man craved one more day of life. With an arrogant smirk, he could face down a 350-pound defensive linebacker intent on crushing him to the turf. Standing up to his billionaire boss/father-in-law took a different kind of courage.

But it was convincing Hayden to go through with the wedding that struck fear in his heart. What if he failed? What if she insisted on going to jail for five years rather than marry him? But as soon as everyone had left the room, Hayden kissed him like she couldn't wait until they consummated their union later tonight. At least he hoped she did. Did she realize what he expected? Desired? Needed? Before he could ask, the butler informed them that Mrs. McQueen had arrived.

An hour later, a bead of sweat broke over his brow as he watched his mother and Hayden together. What were they talking about? He'd told his mother about the engagement, but not the reason behind it.

He'd worried his mother enough over the years, and he'd sworn he'd never be the cause of concern again or a disappointment. Her learning the truth about the pending nuptials would be worse than taking the drink he so desperately craved. His mother was his rock and never gave up on him. Never blamed him when she had every right to.

The two women were of similar height, but his mother had the same reddish-gold curls as her son. Hayden's silky cinnamon-brown mane reminded him of his childhood horse and her blue eyes matched a robin's egg. He wondered what their children might look like. Did she want children?

As Liam watched them, Middleton interrupted the conversation and stole Hayden away. Liam's gut reaction was to follow and protect her. Her father may have signed him when no one else would, but he was a bully with his own daughter, which infuriated Liam. Before he could move, his mother joined him.

"Liam, she may not be the woman I would have pictured you with, but I can tell she loves you."

Hayden deserved an acting award for convincing his mother. But could he live with the lie? "Mom—"

"I like her spunk and honesty."

"What exactly did she tell you?"

"She told me you came to her rescue that night at the bar. And what a gentleman you were afterward. And that how even after you were engaged you wouldn't have sex with her. Hence, tonight's surprise wedding."

If Liam had been drinking, he'd spit out the contents. His Hayden did have spunk and knew exactly what to say to his mother to make her believe.

"Your father would be so proud of you."

Tears welled in his eyes. His father wouldn't be proud.

"Oh, Liam. Don't be upset. He's right here with you."

He choked on his emotions but managed to wrangle the words of apology out. "I'm sorry, Mom."

"Stop that right now, Liam James." She wrapped him up in a hug.

How could such a small woman pack such might into a hug? For a moment he wallowed in the comfort like a five-year-old boy.

"You have nothing to be sorry for." She let go and patted his shoulder before fixing his tie. "This is a happy day."

The urge for a drink slipped away with his mother's words. He smiled so she wouldn't worry any further.

The party was in full swing when Hayden returned with her father. Middleton took the microphone from the band and called Liam up to join them.

Silence filled the room, and Middleton made the surprise announcement. "This isn't a engagement party. It's a wedding."

At first the silence continued as Liam registered the shock on the guests' faces. Did they realize Hayden had no choice? Or did they suspect that the rushed wedding had to do with a surprise pregnancy?

Then Hondo raised up his glass up. "Hey, everyone, Liam's getting laid tonight!"

His teammates joined in with hoots and catcalls. Liam expected Hayden to be mad, but she elbowed him in the ribs and looked up at him with a big smile on her face.

"Okay, let's get started," Judge Mayer said. "I chose these vows with both of Hayden and Liam's pasts in mind."

"Wait!" Hannah grabbed a centerpiece of flowers, shoving them into Hayden's hands.

As they stood in front of Judge Mayer, Liam felt his

father's presence. And his acceptance. A feeling of peace settled into his heart as he repeated the words spoken by the judge.

"I, Liam James McQueen, take you to be my lawfully wedded wife. Before these witnesses I vow to love you and care for you as long as we both shall live."

As the words flowed, he realized he meant every single word. Somewhere along the way he'd fallen in love with Hayden.

"I take you, with all your faults and strengths." Liam paused to gather himself before he choked on the next part. No wonder the judge chose this specific set of vows. Both Liam and Hayden had broken pieces and past sins. So wrong for anyone else, perhaps they were perfect for each other.

"As I offer myself to you with all my faults and strengths," he continued without a hitch. Could he hide his faults from Hayden? "I will help you when you need help and turn to you when I need help. I choose you as the person with whom I will spend my life."

Somehow he'd make this marriage work. Someday Hayden would mean the words she spoke back to him now. One day she would say, "I love you" for real, he vowed. Then they would repeat the Christian vows of marriage in front of God.

Hayden smiled, her eyes filling with tears. He hoped to God they were tears of joy and not some act she was putting on or, worse, tears of sadness.

"I pronounce you husband and wife. You may kiss the bride."

Every cell of Liam's body urged him to pull Hayden

into a bruising kiss. To mark her as his, knowing the vows weren't enough. Instead he took a small step closer and ran his thumb along her chin before tilting it up. Her eyes fluttered closed, and her mouth parted slightly in an almost Scarlett O'Hara fashion. He kissed her tenderly, the way a bride should be kissed.

But tonight he wouldn't hold back. He'd unleash his desire for his bride. She was no virgin and he no saint.

And oddly, the thought brought another sense of peace. Was this God's twisted way of answering his prayer for a partner in life, a wife to share his life with, to grow old with? And, okay, honestly to make love to.

God created Eve for Adam.

And I get Hayden.

He grinned.

The rest of the party passed in a blur as teammates ribbed him about 'tapping that ass' and asked him if he needed any pointers.

He looked at his watch for the hundredth time. *Ten o'clock.* Hoping the hour would be acceptable, he asked, "Want to make our grand exit?"

"Sure," Hayden said, "but there's something important I have to take care of first. Wait here."

While he waited, he said goodbye to his mother. She reassured him that she was being well taken care of by Mr. Middleton. Liam watched with curiosity as Hayden headed to the band with a sheaf of papers.

The music ended mid-beat as she tapped the microphone. "Thank you all for coming to the surprise wedding of the year. I have one thing to do before we head out to consummate this marriage."

Laughter filled the room. His teammates hooted. If his mother's smile was any indication, she was amused by Hayden's antics.

"This is the pre-nup Liam signed." She waved the contract in the air. "And well—"

Hayden couldn't have shocked him more as she tore the papers into small pieces. Liam turned to see her father's reaction. He'd never seen his boss so angry, even after last years Championship loss.

"It must be love," declared a drunken Charlize. The guests followed the mother-of-the-bride's lead and cheered.

Turning back to see Hayden's smile full of triumph, Liam wondered if her stunt was a really a present for him or a power play against her father. She ran off the stage as people clapped. Throwing the pieces of the contract into the air over them like the traditional rice over a newly married couple, she said to him, "Let's go." She grabbed his hand. "Time to make good on those claims you made about your future bride." She gave him that come-hither smile. "Because for better or for worse, I'm her."

Chapter 12

As they drove away from the marina, Hayden examined the wedding band resting on top of her *grand-mère's* engagement ring. How had she let it get this far?

Because I wanted it to.

She glanced at Liam's hand gripping the steering wheel. She noted how the matching band that belonged to her grandfather fit perfectly on her new husband's finger. *Husband? Holy shit!*

"That took balls," Liam said.

"The pre-nup?" When he nodded, she added, "I can assure you I don't have any."

"That's a relief." Liam chuckled.

What had possessed her to tear the pre-nup into confetti? Was it about standing up to her father? If so, was pissing him off worth the money Liam could sue for if they divorced? In her heart she knew Liam's pride would never let him take one dime. Unless her heart was wrong about him, and then she was screwed.

But who turns down five million dollars? She couldn't tell him in words how much his actions meant to her. Liam may not love her, but he stood by her when he could have walked.

Either way, it had felt right in the moment. No, it felt more than right. It felt glorious. She'd live the fairy tale

81

until reality caught up with her.

Wrapped up in her thoughts, she hadn't registered the route Liam was taking.

"Where are we going?"

"My place."

"You think I'm going to live in Tribeca?" Feeling more like herself, she continued, "My place has a view of the park and has actual closets."

"A musician used to own my apartment." He glanced at her. "It's soundproof."

"What difference does that make?"

"I'm going to make you scream, Hayden. Loud. Over and over again."

She involuntarily squirmed, her body throbbing with anticipation. "Then why aren't you driving faster?"

Liam laughed and pressed his foot on the gas.

Reaching the apartment, he fumbled with the keys while Hayden secretly smiled, relieved he was as nervous as she was. She cocked an eyebrow when he waited for her to walk in before him.

"Oh, right." He tossed her over his shoulder.

"That's not the way a groom is supposed to carry his bride over the threshold." She knew it wasn't a real marriage. That this was only for fun, but she still ached for something more.

"No, but it's our way."

"Put me down!"

He did as she requested, but backed her up against the entryway wall as he kicked the door closed. "I can't wait to taste you. Really taste you." His lips descended on hers with a hunger so unlike the chaste kiss he delivered in front of the guests. And so much better.

"I'm going to make you come, Hayden. Right here. Right now."

Catching her breath, she barely registered his words as he dropped to his knees. He tugged off his suit jacket and threw it aside.

"Every time you walk through my door you're going to see this wall and get wet remembering how I made you come." He pushed her dress all the way to her hips. "It turns me on knowing you don't wear panties. I love knowing I'll have easy access to your pussy whenever I want."

"Liam," she panted. It was all she was capable of. Anticipating the warmth of his breath, her pussy slicked with wet heat

His hands drew around to the back of her legs to cup the place where her thighs meant her ass. He inhaled her and then blew a warm breath over her sensitive skin. Tingles lit up every nerve ending, and he hadn't even touched her there yet. Sliding his tongue between her inner lips, he hit the nub, retreating, then back and again in a rocking motion that at any moment would split her insides in half from the intense pleasure of it.

He nudged her thighs wider so he could lap her with his tongue, curling it at just the right moment. His fingers massaged the back of her legs, intensifying the pleasure. He knew exactly how to bring a woman to the brink of madness.

Heat pooled between her thighs, her sex swollen with desire. He increased the pressure of his tongue until she jerked back and her head smacked against the wall. She couldn't come like this. Then she did. She clutched at the wall for support, but there was nothing to hold onto. Her hands landed in his hair. Grabbing a fistful of strands, she tugged him closer. He moaned his approval. The vibration of his mouth sent her into another realm. She let go. Utterly. Completely. Wave upon wave of pleasure pounded through her until she sobbed in relief as the storm ebbed.

He was right. Every time she walked through that door, the memory of this moment would make her body react. And he'd better be ready to do something about it.

Liam licked his lips. "You are delicious."

Hayden gripped his shoulders as he tried to stand. Her thighs trembled from the release. Hell, her whole body felt electrified. "I can't stand on my own."

"No worries." Instead of tossing her over his shoulder, he scooped her up, cradling her in his arms.

"You're going to throw your back out."

Liam smirked. "I could bench press you all day and not break a sweat."

"Oh yeah, well how are you at push-ups?' Hayden wiggled her eyebrows.

"You'll see soon enough."

Liam put her down at the foot of his bed and turned her so her back faced him. He unzipped her dress and kissed the base of her neck. As his mouth glided over her skin, she bit her lip, trying not to moan. He unhooked her bra, one hook at a time, slowly, like he was savoring the moment. She felt his rough fingertips trace a line down her spine as he tugged the long zipper lower, toward her ass and beyond. The dress, which fit perfectly, clung to every curve. She did a little shimmy to free herself of her bra and the clinging fabric.

"Now that is what I call a work of art."

Hayden swiveled on her heel, turning to face him in time to see him yank out of his tie and shirt. "So are your abs," she said. The skin stretched across the planes of his stomach so tightly she bet she could bounce a penny off of it. As he cupped her breasts, she reached for the button of his waistband.

She unzipped his pants and pulled him free. "Now this is built for pleasure." She moved her hand along the length of his cock. "My pleasure." She reveled in the weight of him. She could feel the raw power of him pulse in her hand.

"On the bed, Hayden," he said, his voice tight and his jaw clenched.

Excited to see if he'd lose the control he was so obviously trying to maintain, she crawled up the bed toward the pillows so he could enjoy the view of her ass. She glanced over her shoulder, frozen a moment by his heated gaze, and then she rolled to her back, eager to feel him inside her. She rested her head against the pile of pillows, crooked her finger, and spread her legs in invitation.

"I think I've just seen paradise," he said, kicking off his pants and briefs, his gaze never leaving her.

He made her feel beautiful. Wanted. Desired. Her core ached for him.

He knelt between her open thighs. "You're mine, Hayden." Before she could respond he kissed her fully. His tongue swirled with hers, reminding her of how expertly he'd tongued other parts of her. She squirmed beneath him, urgent for more than kisses.

She loved how his hands handled her body. Masterful. Possessive.

She loved the feel of his hard, muscular body against her soft curves.

She loved the way he worshipped her breasts with his mouth.

She loved. Him.

"Look at me, Hayden."

He held her gaze hostage as he pushed inside her, his size stretching and filling her. Her eyes widened as he hit the spot that only her vibrator seemed to find. "Oh!"

"You feel so good, Hayden." Liam smiled down at her. "This was worth two years of celibacy."

His words struck her deep in her heart while his passionate thrusts drove her wild. He did all the work, yet she was the one breathless. Liam was so hard, so big, she felt him throb inside her or maybe it was she who throbbed. Fused together as one, the lines blurred of where he ended and she began.

She needed air, but she needed him more. Needed the release more than life. Then the first ripple hit her. She tightened around him and she shook with uncontrollable tremors of pleasure. *More and then more.* He drove in harder, riding out her release with his own. Her screams probably set a new decibel level. Thank goodness for his soundproof apartment.

He rolled over, taking her with him. Both hands lovingly explored her ass cheeks. She rested her head on his chest, listening to the frantic beat of his heart that was identical to hers. Did the feelings within him match as well?

Or was it just sex for him? Or worse, payment for

services rendered for being her get-out-of-jail-free card? It didn't feel that way. She felt loved as his one hand followed the curve of her back and the other played with her long hair.

She lifted her head to explore his chest with her lips. "Do you need a time out?"

"Heck, no. I've just gotten back in the game."

She offered a wicked smile. "Then let's play." Hayden couldn't wait to go on offense.

Chapter 13

What a woman.

What a mouth.

Hayden threatened to send him to an early grave. Her lips moved over him in slow, torturous strokes. Maybe, this was his hell. Then she sucked all of him in to the deep recess of her warm, wet mouth. No, this was his heaven.

Her throaty moans fueled the blood rushing to his groin. The cold air hit his cock when her mouth retreated. He fisted his hands so he wouldn't grab her hair like a caveman and push her head back down to finish him off.

She looked up at him, her eyes as luminous as blue flames. "Your cock is so hard. So big."

There it was. The words every man loved to hear. He felt rewarded for not giving into his primal needs. "You made me this hard. This big." He needed relief. He needed to be buried deep inside Hayden again.

The soft flesh of her breasts, the hard peak of her nipples grazed his cock, then his abs, and his chest. Her sleek body rubbed against his like a cat intent on getting attention. He was one touch away from throwing her onto her back and sinking himself into her slick heat.

She purred as she slid her pussy down onto his cock. "I'm glad it was you at Martini Madness, Liam."

But her words were lost to him when she gyrated her

womanly hips, slow and sensual. Hell and heaven all at the same time.

"I'm about to make you very glad too."

Liam hadn't viewed twerking as particularly sexy, but done on top of his shaft? Oh, Holy heaven. A rush of sensation shot through his body. Hayden knew how to rock a cock. And his world.

Knowing he wouldn't last another minute, he placed his thumb on her clit as she continued to ride him hard. "Liam!" Her nails dug into his biceps and she fought to stay upright.

Fighting a losing battle with his control, he felt his balls tighten, ready to come. Mesmerized by the sight of her head thrown back in ecstasy, he didn't. He wanted to watch her fall apart as she used his cock for her pleasure. Her shouts of release sounded like the sweetest music to his ears.

Her movements slowed. Her hands now braced against chest. She came again as he continued to swipe his thumb on her clit. Her exotic scent surrounded him like cloak of desire. The aroma of sex, spice, and a hint of vanilla intoxicated him like an ancient love potion. Liam breathed her in. He wanted to live in that scent. Get lost in it.

He fanned her long hair to rest above each nipple. The word sexy didn't cut it. More like an erotic dream. "Watching you come is the most beautiful sight I've ever seen," he admitted.

Hayden smiled. "Now, its my turn to watch you."

At least sex wasn't going to be a problem in their marriage. It was a better foundation than the contract her father would have between them. And love could be born out of lust. That's what Liam was counting on.

They made love long into the night until Hayden curled up next to him, repeating the words she said earlier, but this time in a whisper. "I'm glad it was you."

So was he.

Chapter 14

There shouldn't be the awkward morning-after when you're married. Yet that's exactly how Hayden was feeling. Awkward. Unsure. Vulnerable. Should she sneak out of bed and out the door to avoid Liam? Tonight she could return, pretending as if he hadn't tilted her world on its axis.

That would be the coward's way out, and she was not a coward. Besides, she'd be thinking about the awkwardness all day, which would defeat the purpose of escaping. Better to get it over with it. Since she'd marry him all over again, she shouldn't be having regrets.

Hayden poked the body sprawled out next to her.

"What?" Liam grunted.

Yeah, what Hayden? "Um, don't you have to be at practice?"

"Coach said, take the morning off. A wedding present."

"Hmph, what did I get?"

"You got five orgasms."

And didn't he sound so smug about that. And sexy too.

His eyes shot opened. "Want another?" he asked.

"Another five?" Hayden challenged, her pulse already speeding up at the idea.

"Greedy, minx." His eyes closed. "Now you get none."

Ha! Two could play this game. Hayden smacked his

cute ass but resisted the urge to explore the muscular contours. She imagined them together at her apartment instead. His bedroom may be soundproof, but hers had a mirrored ceiling. Her blood heated at the thought of watching that butt in motion as it pumped in and out of her.

"Was that a fly?" he asked.

"A fly?" This time she smacked him with all her might.

"Ow!" He reached out for her, but she scooted off the bed, scooped up last-night's dress, and dashed into the bathroom.

After a leisurely shower, she strolled into the walk-in closet attached to the bathroom and helped herself to a plain black dress shirt. With the sleeves rolled-up and knotted at the waist, Liam's shirt transformed her white satin dress into daytime wear.

In the bedroom he was wide-awake with his head propped up on the pillows. She stopped. God, he look so sexy, laid out and naked, morning erection ready for her to jump onto for a ride.

"What, no breakfast in bed?" he asked.

"Remember, I don't cook." Hayden put her hands on her hips. "But maybe, if I had that orgasm this morning, you would have rated coffee."

"You're the one who jumped out of bed."

"You're the one who didn't follow me into the shower."

"That smack was an invitation?"

Hayden nodded.

"Wow, I'm rusty." Liam scratched the scruff on his chin.

Far from it, Hayden thought.

"You look nice. What are your plans today?"

Nice? She grabbed her earrings and slid them in. "Shenanigans. Mayhem. Hijinks. The usual."

"Hayden."

She stuck out her tongue at his disapproving look. "Oh relax. I do have an actual business to run. Oh, by the way, I'm traveling to Japan next week for the worldwide release of my perfume, Sinfully Mine."

"Yes, you are. All mine. Do you have security detail going with you?"

"A bodyguard. Big and cute."

"Is he neutered?"

A secret part of her relished his jealous tone. "That would be unfair to womankind," she teased.

He shot out of bed. Pulling her into his arms, he said. "It's not a joke." His lips crushed her mouth in a bruising kiss.

There was nothing seductive or sensual, only pure possession. Her traitorous body responded by melting into him.

"Your mine now, Mrs. Hayden McQueen."

Her first reflex was to rebel, but he kissed her again and oh how his kisses turned her insides out and her outside in. 'Hyphenated," she conceded when he finaly let her breathe.

"No." He reached up her skirt fingering her to draw out her liquid heat.

"Liam," she gasped.

His two fingers pumped in while his thumb rubbed her clit. "This belongs to me, Hayden."

My heart does too, she wanted to cry out. Instead she

shattered into a million pieces. Safe in Liam's grip, the pieces of her floated back like a giant shifting jigsaw puzzle, creating something new within her. No, it was more than the sex or even the strength of her orgasm—it was as if the missing parts of her had found their way home.

The morning-after turned out not to be awkward at all. It was way worse. She'd prefer awkward to this scary need for Liam's touch. His kiss. His love. Hayden should have escaped when she had the chance.

"Now, go make me coffee, wife." Liam spanked her bottom then headed for the bathroom, leaving her to admire his bare ass.

Either the orgasm had addled her brain or she was in love for real because damn if she didn't make him coffee, smiling like an idiot the whole time.

Chapter 15

After a short day of practice, Liam stood in the middle of his living room in disbelief. Clothes, purses and enough shoes to outfit a small nation lay strewn about his apartment. Their apartment, he amended. He snagged a lacey teddy with two fingers to examine it. How, with all the ribbons and ties, did the contraption go on? It didn't matter since there was only one way it was going to come off. Torn to shreds with his bare hands. He hated to think how much money she'd wasted on it.

"You're not thinking of trying that on?"

He looked up to see an amused Hayden dressed in tight black leggings and one of his shirts. Even with all her things here, she still chose to wear something of his. *Interesting.* "I'm thinking you need more lingerie and less shoes."

She folded her arms. "Spoken like a true man."

"I am what I am."

They stared at each other for a moment, neither knowing what came next. They had an amazing connection in the bedroom, but Liam was determined to capture that magic and inject it into non-bedroom activities.

"How was practice?"

"Brutal." Liam followed Hayden's lead, though he wasn't one for small talk. "How was your day?"

"I got some strange looks for wearing what turned out to be my wedding dress to an advertising meeting, but I'm used to strange looks." Hayden picked up a few articles of clothing. "What about you? Did your teammates ride your ass about ending your celibacy?"

"Some," he said vaguely. She didn't need to know the full extent of the ribbing.

"Did you tell them I was the best you ever had?"

"I told them to shut the fuck up."

Hayden looked shocked and then laughed uneasily. "I'm sure it wasn't the first time there was a crude remark about me in that locker room."

Liam winced, remembering the coarse jokes thrown around at Hayden's expense in the past. More than once, he'd fought the instinct to punch a teammate. Today he had put an end to the jokes.

"That was before the wedding," he said, seizing the opportunity to show a benefit to their marriage beyond sex.

Hayden clutched her chest. "My hero." She walked over to him and gently took the teddy away. "Though I do have a complaint."

"Let me guess." Liam looked around the room. "I don't have enough closet space?"

"That goes without saying. I'm talking about the fact that you haven't kissed me hello yet."

Her sulky pout begged to be nipped at. Heck, her whole body begged for his mouth. But his cock urged him to skip the foreplay and start the action mid-game.

"Let me remedy that." Instead of kissing her, he picked her up and made his way to the bedroom. Laughing at her squeals of delight, he tossed Hayden onto the pile of clothes on his bed. Their bed, he amended.

"Liam, everything will wrinkle."

"Do you want sex, woman, or to hang up clothes?"

The feline grin of hers made him want to pounce.

"Sex."

"Correct answer." Liam stripped off her clothes and added them to the mess, then quickly added his.

By the time they came up for air, half the clothes were on the floor and the other half surrounded them like a cocoon. What emerged was something beautiful yet still so fragile.

Hayden stretched her sleek body against his, sighing her contentment. He felt confident the last thing she was thinking about was his lack of closet space.

Chapter 16

After the epic clothing sex romp, they lounged on his comfy couch, wearing robes and ate Chinese food right out of the cartons, sometimes feeding each other their favorite dish like a doting couple. Could something based on a lie and lust morph into true love?

Hayden had always scoffed at the idea of falling in love. The most anyone could hope for was great sex and great company. Love belonged to the poets and to the fools of this world. Her belief wavered when she remembered her grandparent's great love for one another.

She placed an empty carton of moo shu pork on the Craftsman coffee table. She smiled, thinking the table was so Liam. Natural, sturdy and made to last.

Stalling, she reached for the fried rice. Liam seemed to love her curves, so she took a couple of more bites. She had yet to bring up the business deal proposed to her earlier today. He wouldn't like it, and she was reluctant to ruin the moment. She tugged at her bottom lip in indecision.

"I know I'm going to regret this, but what's up?" he asked.

How did he know she'd been working up enough nerve to ask him a question?

"Well." She paused, bracing herself for the upcoming

fight. "I got a call today from the producer of *Hayden's Place*. They want us to revive the show."

"Us?"

She nodded.

"Count me out. The team is depending on me to get them back to the Championship. I can't afford another distraction." His chiseled jaw set in stony determination.

Hayden wouldn't give up that easily. "So I'm a distraction? An inconvenience?"

"Nice try, but I'm not your father. Don't put words in my mouth." He put down the remains of the quart of boneless spare ribs. "Why would you want to do it in the first place?"

"It's good for business. Sales skyrocket. I make millions. We make millions."

He sat back and looked up to the ceiling as if searching for answers, or maybe he was saying a silent prayer. Hayden couldn't be sure.

"Did you see the front cover of *People* today? *Squeaky Clean McQueen Marries Troubled Heiress.* Apparently, our nuptials are one of the signs of the coming Apocalypse."

His voice remained calm and cool, irritating Hayden.

"So what? I thought you didn't want to change me. You said I could be myself around you. Be real." She threw his words back at him, hurt that the press thought she wasn't good enough for him. Even though their marriage was a fraud.

He turned his head and looked her in the eye. "How is playing up to a camera real? It's all phony. Done on purpose to make you look bad."

She had no good answer to this. Half of the things she

did for the show were set up and scripted. "That's why people watch. Ratings are the name of the game."

"There's something more to this. What is driving you? It's not just the money."

"I happen to like money."

"You sound like your father." Liam paused. "Do you think the size or your bank account will win his approval?"

"I do not have daddy issues."

"Or do you want to do it to piss him off. Like ripping up the pre-nup."

"Whatever." Let Liam think the worse. If he wanted to throw her goodwill gesture back in her face, then fine.

"Hayden, you do know that your father loves you."

She was so not going there. "You're telling me I can't do the show?"

"I never said *you* couldn't do it." Liam sighed, as if signaling giving up that part of the argument. "But I'm asking you to respect my privacy." He ran a hand through his unruly hair. "To respect our marriage."

To respect our marriage? Did Liam want to make this work too or was he only interested in protecting his image?

The producer wanted both of them, so if he was out, then she was too. "But people will forget about me." She hated the whine in her voice.

"Impossible, Hayden." Liam traced her jawline with his thumb, tilting her chin so she would look him in the eye. "You are unforgettable."

His hands drifted down to where her robe gaped. He pulled the lapels open to access her breasts, cupping each one. "I want to spend the rest of the night memorizing your body with my hands." He brushed a kiss on her lips.

"Then with my mouth."

"After you're done, there will be a test."

Liam raised a brow. "What kind of test?"

"A blindfolded one," she whispered.

"Sounds like my kind of test." He nodded with approval. "But I'll have to examine you thoroughly so I can ace it."

Hayden forgot all about the reality show as he discarded her robe and laid her back onto the cushions. Liam was real, The feel of his hands tenderly mapping her body was real. The love in her heart was real.

Chapter 17

The team rolled to a 3 and 1 record. Liam, back in the good graces of the press and the fans, should be happy. With Hayden away on business and him back from an away game, he loafed on the couch, flipping aimlessly through the channels. He should try to catch up on some much-needed sleep. He avoided the bed, filled with Hayden's scent, but so cold and lonely without her sexy, voluptuous body to warm it. She traveled for business more than she was home, and he wasn't any better with away games.

Liam missed his wife.

Really missed her.

His apartment, now filled with Hayden's things, felt empty without her laughter. He wanted to share stories of the latest win, and then hear about her day of wheeling and dealing. How had she inserted herself into his life so seamlessly? Like she'd belonged there all along.

Hypersensitive to the unusual quiet, he heard the door open despite the television telling him he should buy a new car.

"You're home," he said with way too much enthusiasm. Liam knew he should keep his real feelings buried until Hayden fell in love with him.

"Surprise!" She jumped on his lap just as excited.

"A beautiful surprise." To heck with being cool. He threaded his hands through her hair, covering her lips with his. Tongues mingled in a sensuous play of who missed whom the most.

She pulled away, her eyes now a dreamy blue. "I thought you'd be sleeping. I was planning to wake you in a most delicious manner."

"I can pretend to be asleep." He closed his eyes and snored.

"Too late. You're already hard." She rocked her hips, her sex deliciously rubbing up against his cock, furthering his agony. She leaned forward and whispered into his ear, "And I'm so wet."

That did it. He was in no mood for foreplay. "Bed. Now."

"Race you. Loser gets tied up." Hayden hopped off his lap for a good head start.

"Cheater," he yelled, pretending to dash after her. He'd let her win. Because being a loser in this game was a win for him.

By the time she had him naked and tied, Liam was ready to tear the bonds that held him. Her designer scarves would suffer the same fate as her lingerie if he chose. Instead he savored each brush of her fingertips, enjoyed the torture of each swipe of her tongue, and grew harder with every dirty word out of her sweet, hot mouth.

"Did you miss this, Hayden?" *Did you miss me as much as I missed you?*

"Desperately," she breathed. She loosened the knots. "Make love to me, Liam."

A banging knock at his apartment door jolted Liam awake. The spot beside him was empty of Hayden's lovely form. He glanced at the clock. 3:00 a.m. Who the hell could it be?

He jumped out of bed, slid into a pair of sweatpants, and then heard a muffled male voice. A former boyfriend? A current one? No, that was the late hour talking. He took a calming breath before jealousy overrode his good sense. Hayden had never given him any reason to suspect she'd been unfaithful.

Stepping into the hallway, he listened to the voices coming from the living room. Liam didn't like to eavesdrop, but Hayden was his wife and, while her business was her business in the light of a day, at 3:00 a.m. it was his.

"Harry, it's the middle of the night." she said. "Can't this wait until tomorrow?"

Liam rested his forehead on the wall in relief. Not a former boyfriend, just her pompous younger brother. Before the wedding, Liam had only met him a couple of times, but each encounter had left a bitter taste in his mouth. His opinion of Harry hadn't improved. A sense of entitlement radiated from the spoiled brat.

"You have to help me," Harry told his sister.

"What happened this time?" Hayden asked.

In a rush, Harry explained his car had been impounded for outstanding tickets. Of course that wasn't the worst of it—five grams of cocaine would most likely be discovered at any moment. Harry wanted his sister to take the fall. Again?

"We'll say you borrowed my car to avoid the press. It

worked the last time."

What last time? Had Hayden covered for her brother last year? She'd spent three months in rehab and completed a hundred hours of community service for that conviction.

"I can't do it Harry. I just got off of probation. I'll go to jail."

"You have to. You'll get away with it. You always do. Judge Mayer loves you now that you married choirboy McQueen."

Liam clenched his fists, fighting the urge to pommel her brother. Stepping out of the shadows, he said, "You heard her the first time. The answer is no."

Chapter 18

Hayden's heart stopped at the protective but fierce expression on Liam's face.

In a scathing tone, Harry said, "This is none of your concern. Family only."

She'd never seen such a hateful look from Harry. Her eyes widened in shock. Where was her sweet little brother?

Before Hayden could blink an eye, Liam had placed himself between them. "I'm her husband. That makes me family."

"That's what you think," Harry snarled.

"What does that mean?" She took Liam's hand. That he considered them family gave her hope. Perhaps their marriage was more than a sham.

Harry took a step toward her, stumbling over his words. "You didn't even want him on the team, never mind in your bed. He's a loser, remember?"

"Liam, I—"

"That not breaking news." He patted her hand. "The fact that you've covered for your brother's ass is."

"Not anymore." For the first time she saw her little brother for what he was—a drug addict. "Harry, I'll be there to support you, but I won't enable you any longer. You need professional help. Rehab."

His lip curled into a sneer. "Look at you, all high and

mighty. You get a ring and now you're Suzie-fucking-homemaker."

Hayden's eyes watered. Her brother had never lashed out like that at her. It must be the drugs.

"You will not talk to your sister like that."

She was glad Liam was here. In the business world she was known as a piranha, but when it came to her brother, she was like a protective mama bear.

"You'll regret not helping me." Harry headed to the door. "You both will."

"Harry—" But the door slammed before she could reason with him. "My father is going to be livid."

"But not with you."

"Yes, with me." Hayden folded her arms. "He'll accuse me of being a bad influence on my brother. I gave him his first beer. Introduced him to the club scene."

"Like he wouldn't have done those things on his own? Even if that were true, Hayden, your brother is an adult. He's responsible for his own choices."

"My father doesn't see it that way."

"He doesn't know what you did for Harry. Why did you take the fall for him?"

"With those angelic looks? He would not survive jail."

"And you would?"

"Better me than him." She shrugged. "My father will be devastated. He loves Harry."

"Hayden, he loves you too."

"Whatever." No matter what she accomplished, she'd never been the apple of her father's eye. Even knowing football inside and out hadn't impressed him. Harry was the golden child. The favorite.

"No, not whatever," Liam said. "Do you know what your father told me when I argued that our engagement would hurt the team's chances for a Championship run?"

Fearing Liam's answer, she went on the defensive. "Oh, I don't know. That you didn't have a snowball's chance of getting back there anyway."

"No." Liam's mouth tilted a notch upwards into a soft smile. "He said 'my daughter is more important than any Championship.'"

"He said that?" Tears flowed freely from her eyes. Her father loved her? He'd never said the words. Neither had she. To anyone.

Engulfed in Liam's strong embrace, his warmth blanketed more than just her body. Her heart had found a place to shelter.

She'd gone from wanting to get out of their fake engagement to wanting to do everything in her power to make sure, that one day, they celebrated their sixtieth anniversary, just like her grandparents.

Hopefully, she'd have more success with keeping Liam, than she'd had with getting rid of him.

Chapter 19

The darkened room suited Liam's mood today, the anniversary of the worst day of his life. A reminder of all he'd lost and all he had to atone for. Glancing at his phone, he saw his mother's name. He knew that she was hurting just as much as he was. But how could he comfort her when he was to blame for her misery? He answered her call only because she would worry more if he didn't.

"How are you, Liam?"

"I'm fine. I'm not drinking." *Yet.* A sealed bottle of Scotch sat before him on the coffee table, tempting him to accept numbness over grief. "How are you?"

"I visited your father's grave."

Liam's eyes filled. He'd only cried twice in his life. The day his father died and the day he asked God to reenter his heart. "I'll visit after the season."

"You can visit with him whenever you want. Speak to him."

"I know. I do." He choked out the words.

"Are you okay? Where's Hayden?"

Liam still stared at the bottle. "Yeah, Mom. No worries. Hayden is at a business meeting. She'll be home soon." Then somehow, he'd have to pretend like he hadn't lost his best friend four years ago. "I love you, Mom."

"I love you too. I'll see you once the season is over.

Call me if you need anything."

He smiled for the first time that day. He guessed mothers never stopped being moms. "No, you call me if you need anything."

As he ended the call, Hayden entered the living room. He hadn't heard the door or her footsteps. There was no time to hide the Scotch. Maybe it was better that she knew what she was really up against.

"What's going on, Liam?" she said slowly like she was trying to gage the situation.

"I didn't have a drink."

"I didn't say that you did." She tossed her purse to a chair. "Why do you want one? Is it something I did?"

"No, Hayden. Come here." Her desperate plea ate away at his heart. When she sat down next to him, he ran a reassuring hand down her hair. He touched his forehead to hers. "There's nothing you could do to make me want to take a drink."

"Then why? I thought things were good. With us, and the team is 7 and 2."

He pulled away. "I don't want to talk about it." If she knew, it would change everything.

"That's not fair, Liam. You helped me with Harry, but I can't help you? What about our vows? 'I will help you when you need help, and turn to you when I need help'."

She was right. If they were to have a true marriage, he should turn to his wife when he needed help, just as Hayden let him support her. It couldn't be one-sided. Besides, she deserved to know what a mess he was. "My dad died four years ago today."

Her hand flew to her chest and her eyes widened. "Oh

Liam. I'm sorry I didn't know today was the... I should know that. I'm a terrible wife."

"Hayden, stop. You're a wonderful wife."

"I am?"

Poor Hayden, she was always looking for approval when she had nothing to prove. "Yes. You are." He stroked her cheek. "I'm sorry you had to see me like this."

"There's more. Tell me. I can see you're torturing yourself."

Liam took a deep breath and dragged his fingers down his face. "My father is dead because of me."

"Your father died in a car accident. A drunk driver."

"That's the ironic part." Disgusted, he smacked the bottle off the table, and it crashed to the carpeted floor. *Unbreakable.* Unlike his will to resist temptation. "He was driving to Arizona to confront me about my drinking. An intervention."

Hayden moved from the sofa to the coffee table, blocking his view of where the bottle had landed. Taking both of his hands, she said, "That still doesn't make it your fault."

"It is, Hayden. If I had been a better Christian, then he would have never been on that road in the first place. It's easy to be a Christian when everything is going good. After I went pro, I got sick of everyone from the fans to the press, questioning my faith, hoping I would fail. And I did. I started to lose. Badly. The first time I was tested with adversity, I failed, turning to alcohol and women instead of God. Then my father got killed."

"And your grief made things worse," Hayden said.

As if that were any excuse.

"I hit bottom. The bottom of the last bottle, that is. That night, I fell to the floor in a hotel room, cursing God. Then I passed out. When I woke up, the Bible stared at me from underneath the bed. I couldn't believe it. I reached for it and read and read until I asked God to enter my heart. At that exact moment my phone rang. It was my agent. I asked for help. I was in rehab within two hours."

"Liam, it's not your fault. Your father wouldn't want you to blame yourself."

"It is my fault." He swiped the wetness from his face. "My father's death was God's punishment for my sins. I don't deserve to be forgiven."

"I'll admit I don't know a lot about Christianity, but isn't forgiveness one of the main tenets of the faith?"

Liam nodded, glad that she wasn't mentioning his tears.

"And that includes forgiving yourself?"

"It does. I'll work on that, promise. Thank you, Hayden."

"Is there anything I can do to help you through this?"

"You already have." He squeezed her hand. "But this is a battle only I can win. Recovery is an inside job."

"Um, at the risk of hellfire and brimstone being rained down on me, why don't we take a walk down the block? There's a church around the corner. Catholic, I think. We could light a candle for your father."

"I'm not Catholic." Liam laughed for the second time that day. "But I don't think they would mind." It's probably something he should do every year or come up with another way to deal with his father's death. Find some way to honor his life, instead of wallowing in his death. "I have to do something first."

He picked up the bottle, took it to the kitchen sink, and opened the cap. The sweet smell of booze wafted up, and his resolve wavered for a moment. Hayden stood beside him, her scent of spice and vanilla more intoxicating than any alcohol. The comfort of her words outmatched the brief relief any tumbler of Scotch ever could.

She wasn't the spoiled heiress everyone thought she was, but from this day on, he'd spoil her with love. The words sprang to his lips, but he didn't say them yet. To tell Hayden now that he was in love with her wouldn't be fair. His declaration would forever be attached to this sad day. Hayden deserved more than that. In fact, she deserved a real proposal. Would she say yes?

He tilted the bottle. The amber liquid swirled down the drain just like his life had once gone down the pipes. But today he was sober, another day won.

Now he needed to win his wife.

Chapter 20

Exhausted, Hayden slumped against the elevator wall. With Harry in rehab, she was left to pick up the pieces of his division at Middleton Nuts, while still juggling her candied-nuts division, her own business, and her charity work, not to mention being the wife of the top-rated quarterback in the league. Now 12 and 2, the team was primed to sail into the playoffs.

The disappointment in Liam's voice when she canceled their dinner date earlier echoed hers. Hayden hoped he understood that it was only temporary until Harry was ready to take back his responsibilities. Her assistant, Judith, had really stepped up her game, and Hayden planned on delegating more once everything was back to normal.

The elevator door opened and she trudged to the front door.

Maybe she'd take a long vacation once the season was over so she could enjoy time off with Liam. Maybe think about having a baby. *Wow, where did that come from?* The thought of creating a child with him excited and scared her. He'd be a great father, she knew, but how would she do as a mother?

She chewed on her lip. Perhaps if she did the opposite of everything her parents had done, she'd be okay. She unlocked the door and turned the handle. The wall inside still had the small dent from when she threw back her head in ecstasy on their wedding night. Liam called it his trophy wall and refused to have it fixed.

"Hey, beautiful."

She blushed like a pre-teen instead of a married woman of three months. But there was nothing innocent about the way Liam's warm smile heated her insides. He gave her a quick kiss. Too quick for her liking.

Handing her a glass of red wine, he said, "Merlot. I figured you'd like a glass before dinner."

"But—"

"Just because I have a problem doesn't mean you should deny yourself. You need to unwind."

He maneuvered her into the candlelit living room. Jazz played low in the background. In no time he had her reclining on the couch, shoes off, and her feet in his lap. She took a sip of the wine. *Ahh.*

He massaged her tired feet with hands worth millions on the field. She relaxed into the cushions, releasing the day's worries from her mind and body. "I think my feet are going to have an orgasm."

Liam laughed. "You can show me your undying gratitude later."

"Oh, I will," she said as he continued to rub her feet. She considered asking him to move his hands a little higher up her legs. Like all the way up, to work his talented fingers on her pussy.

"Hayden?"

"Hmmm…?"

"I—"

Her dreaded cell phone buzzed. She didn't care if Middleton Nuts was on fire, she was not answering. Then Liam's phone rang.

"It's my agent," he said.

Her cell continued to buzz. She peeked at the screen with one eye. "My assistant."

"Might be important."

While Liam left the room to take his call, with a sigh she answered her own phone. "What's up, Judith?"

"I'm sorry to bother you at home, but…" Her assistant hesitated on the other end of the line.

"But what?"

"That reporter Ender called looking for a statement."

"A statement about what?" All the tension Liam worked out of her body returned. What could possibly be wrong now? She'd been good. Very good. And very happy.

"Ender's writing a story about your husband that claims your marriage isn't legal. He's calling it "The Saint Living in Sin.' Ender says he has a source."

"Who?"

"He's not saying. Ender discovered your marriage documents haven't been filed with the City Clerk's Office. There's no record of your marriage."

"That's ridiculous. Judge Mayer presided over the ceremony." Hayden heard her voice rise with each word. She'd never had yelled at an employee before. "I'm so sorry. I'm not yelling at you."

"I understand. I'd be upset too."

Hayden was fuming. Was Liam receiving the same news from his agent? She instructed Judith to issue a "no comment" statement until they could figure out what was going on.

But when Liam walked back in to join her, he was whistling like he didn't have a care in the world. Was he happy to learn they weren't married? Or had his agent called about something else?

He hadn't.

"How can you whistle at a time like this?" she demanded, pacing the living room.

"Hayden, it's a technicality. The judge is a busy man."

"No, my father had a hand in this." Her panic rose with each step. "I tore up the pre-nup so he destroyed the marriage license. Harry must have seen him do it." She stopped. "Harry said we would regret not helping him. This must be what he meant. How could he do this to me?"

"Harry must have spoke to Ender before he went into rehab." Liam enfolded her in his arms. "People do crazy stuff when they're addicts. Who am I to judge? I think Harry deserves a second chance too."

"But what are we going to do?" she sniffed against his chest. They weren't married. Liam would kick her out and be done with her and her screwed-up family.

"Nothing."

"Nothing?" she screeched out.

"It's just a piece of paper." He held her chin and tilted it up so their gazes met. "In my heart we're married."

Did that mean he wanted to be married? Did it mean he loved her? Hope burned in her heart.

"I meant every word I said to you that day, Hayden. And I mean them more each day. I hope you do too."

"I do. I love you Liam." She stood on her tippy-toes and kissed him with all the love in her heart. She pulled away first. "But what about your reputation as a Christian, your vow of celibacy until you married? We're living in sin."

He stroked her cheek. "God knows what was in my heart that day." He pressed her hand to his chest. "He knows what's in it now. But I can see that you don't."

Liam guided her to the couch and sat her down. *What's happening?* When he got down on one knee, her heart fluttered wildly, trying to escape the confines of her chest to hand itself over to him. *My husband is about to propose!*

"As I was about to say before we got interrupted—" He pulled a ring case from his pocket and opened it.

She didn't look, not even a peek, because the light in his eyes already held the sparkle of a whole diamond mine.

"I love you, Hayden. Marry me. For real. Forever."

"Yes, yes!" Unable to contain her happiness, she jumped up, nearly knocking the ring out of his hand.

Her hands shook as she slipped off her *grand-mère's* ring and put it on her right hand. Liam replaced it with a princess-cut diamond sparkler. "It's beautiful," she said, her breath catching in her throat.

The number of carats didn't match the ring bequeathed to her, but that didn't matter. The man who stood before her, looking into her eyes was beyond any price. "When did you buy this?"

"A couple of days ago. Figured our three-month wedding anniversary was a good time to propose to you."

"What are we going to do about the press? They'll be brutal once Ender's story breaks."

"We'll leak it to the press that your father didn't want us to marry, that he pretended to relent by hosting the ceremony, fooling us into thinking it was the real deal. Our tale of star-crossed lovers will keep the tabloids busy right through the playoffs."

"And here I thought you didn't have a sneaky bone in your body."

"Well, the Quarterback Sneak is my specialty."

"No, it's not." She laughed. "I happen to know it's going deep."

Liam raised a brow. "Practice makes perfect."

"Then let's hit the field," she said, leading him to their bed.

Epilogue

Hayden gazed at the azure blue of the ocean stretched out before her. The breeze billowed her silk robe around her legs. Peace filled her soul, love filled her heart, and her body was sated to the point of numbness.

"Admit it. You're going crazy," Liam said from the king-size bed.

"That was a sigh of contentment."

"Liar."

She turned to face him. "Okay, so it's strange not having a camera in my face 24-7."

"You may not be able to tweet from the island, but…" Liam picked up his phone from the nightstand and wiggled it in the air. "I could film you doing naughty things to me."

Her eyes widened. "A sex tape? With everything I've done, I have never gone *there*."

"You could make millions," he teased.

"We have millions." But how could she resist such a tempting offer? "We could release it when we're like ninety. Shock the hell out of our great-grandchildren."

"I have a feeling they won't be so shocked."

"Probably not." Hayden giggled then turned serious. Untying the knot of her robe, she let the silky fabric skim over her to pool at her feet. Goosies pricked across her skin as she anticipated Liam's rough hands gliding over her body.

"Ready for your close-up, Mrs. McQueen?" Liam pointed the phone at her.

She approached the bed, swaying her hips like a forties' starlet. "I was born ready."

But made just for you.

Thank you for taking the time to read The Quarterback Sneak.

If you enjoyed it, please consider telling your friends or posting a short review. Word of mouth is an author's best friend and much appreciated.

About the Author

Liz Matis is a mild mannered accountant by day and romance author by night. Married 29 years she believes in happily-ever-after!

Fun Fact: Liz read her first romance at the age of fifteen and soon after wrote her first romances starring her friends and their latest crushes!

Fun Fact 2: Liz kept an inspiration board for The Quarterback Sneak on Pinterest. Check it out here:
www.pinterest.com/lizmatis/

Keep in Touch with Liz

Website:
http://www.lizmatis.com

Blog:
http://www.taoofliz.blogspot.com

Email:
elizabethmatis@gmail.com

Twitter:

@LizMatis

Facebook:

Liz Matis Fan Page

Goodreads:
www.goodreads.com/author/show/5289185.Liz_Matis

The Wives of Fantasy Football Romance Blog:
www.wivesoffantasyfootballromance.blogspot.com

To sign up for my newsletter please contact Liz at:
elizabethmatis@gmail.com

Read Samantha And Ryan's story…

Playing For Keeps ("Fantasy" Football – Season 1) by Liz Matis

Winner of the NECRWA First Kiss Contest

Journalist Samantha Jameson always wanted to be one of the boys, but

Ryan Terell won't let her join the club.

Ryan Terell is a playmaker on and off the field, but when Samantha uncovers his moves, he throws out the playbook. Just as he claims his sweetest victory, Samantha's investigation into a steroid scandal involving his team forces him to call a time-out to their off the record trysts. But then a life threatening injury on the field will force them both to decide just how far they'll go to win the game.

Read Hannah and Jake's story…

Going For It ("Fantasy" Football – Season 2) by Liz Matis

Pro football player Jake Miller's game plan for winning back supermodel Hannah Hahn is play action in the bedroom. Once he sees beyond the swimsuits and lingerie, feelings of love blindside him, changing the rules of the game.

Hannah owns the runway, but that success came with a price and a secret that's kept her from trusting a man until Jake crashes through her defenses.

The paparazzi love the beauty and the beast couple but the tabloid rumors turn ugly and test the fragile trust between them. Then Hannah loses an ad campaign to fashion's new 'it' girl. Her desperate reaction will cause Jake to challenge everything she's ever believed about herself.

Read Angel and Billy's story...

Huddle Up ("Fantasy" Football – Season 3) by Liz Matis

When Angel O'Malley is left penniless by her deceased father's gambling debts, she is forced to sue pro football player Billy Burner for child support. Blindsided with a five-year-old daughter, he tackles fatherhood with the same commitment he gives to the game, but he has his eye on a bigger prize: Angel's heart.

She agrees to Billy's plan to play house to ensure the new father makes no rookie mistakes. Though their passions burn hotter than ever they must overcome old betrayals, past hurts, and new insecurities if they are to prevent history from repeating itself.

Can a long ago summer love turn into an everlasting one?

Also:

Love By Design by Liz Matis

Design Intervention starts the second season with its own surprise makeover. Interior designer Victoria Bryce must break in her temporary co-host, Aussie Russ Rowland.

Sparks fly on camera as they argue over paint colors and measurement mishaps leading to passions igniting behind the scenes. But when their pasts collide with the present will the foundation they built withstand the final reveal? An HGTV meets Sex and the City romp!

Real Men Don't Drink Appletinis by Liz Matis

Hollywood's handsomest men surround celebrity agent Ava Gardner but none are as intriguing as larger-than-life Grady O'Flynn. The Navy SEAL is on an unsanctioned mission when they end up starring in their own romantic comedy.

Will they continue to sizzle when Grady has to report back to duty? In this sexy novelette by Liz Matis, two lovers have two weeks to find out.

Coming Soon:

Summer Dreaming – Summer 2015